Abducted

Hilda Stahl

Cover Illustration by Ed French

**bethel
publishing**
1819 S. Main, Elkhart, IN 46516

DEDICATED WITH LOVE
to
Richard Oltz—the great editor and friend
and to
Mary Oltz who loves a hot fudge sundae
as well as a mystery

SPECIAL THANKS
to
Marcelle Birta

Chapter 1

Sweat broke out on his forehead and above his upper lip. He gripped the steering wheel tightly as the little girl ran across her yard and down the sidewalk. Leaning against the wheel, he groaned. The pain in his gut was as powerful as when the prison doors slammed on him. He shouldn't be here watching the girl. It would get him in trouble. Maybe as much trouble as the last time he'd watched a little girl.

He closed his eyes for a moment. It wouldn't be the same this time. No! It wouldn't be!

He nodded. He would only watch her and enjoy the way her blond hair streamed out behind her as she ran to school. He wouldn't touch her. He wouldn't lose control. Not this time, he wouldn't. "I won't hurt her," he whispered. "I promise."

He plucked at his carefully trimmed beard, then slowly pulled away from the curb and followed the girl. She stopped at the crosswalk to watch a robin fly into a budding tree. He watched it too until it flew out of sight behind a white house with peeling paint. The robin was a good sign. It might even be an omen. Maybe his luck was changing and from this day forward he'd be happy and loved. "Happy and loved. Happy and loved," he whispered as he rocked gently with the motion of his words.

Brushing the sweat from his forehead, he dabbed his thin mustache and carefully followed a red pickup to the school. The pickup drove on but he parked at the curb. He watched the girl run down the sidewalk toward him. His heart thudded painfully.

He had to speak to her! That's all he would do—speak—and then let her run into the school building.

He stepped from his car and the girl stopped and stared at him. Oh, what wide blue eyes she had! She studied him and he could see that she was wondering if she knew him. She had seen him several times in the past three weeks that he had been following her.

"Hello," he said with a smile as he stepped to the sidewalk.

She swallowed hard and darted a look toward the school. She wanted to run past him, but couldn't without going close to him. Maybe he was dad's friend. Maybe that's where she had seen him before. "Hello." She sounded hesitant. Tilting her head, she looked up at him again.

Abruptly he shoved his hands into his jacket pockets to keep from touching her shiny blond hair. "My name is Sam," he said.

"Do you know my dad?" She fingered the tiny bear in her jacket pocket.

He didn't but he smiled and nodded. "We're good friends. He told me your name, but I forgot it. Now, isn't that terrible, forgetting your name? What would your dad think of me?" Sam smiled but his stomach tightened into a cold, hard ball. He must let her go now or he couldn't stop himself from caressing her baby-fine hair.

A breeze blew her lightweight blue jacket away from her thin body. Shouts and laughter rang from the front door of the school where several walkers waited for the doors to be opened.

"Ann," the girl finally said. "My name is Ann Louise Hewitt. I'm nine. Did Dad tell you that?"

"Ann." Slowly he reached out and stroked her soft, flowing hair. "He told me a lot of things about you."

"I miss him a lot. I didn't want him to leave me and Mom." Ann moved just enough so that his hand fell away from her.

Sam shot a look toward the school and then glanced over his shoulder to his car. His pulse raced and sweat popped out again on his forehead. Could he get her to his car?

What was he thinking? It could put him in jail again.

But how could it? He wouldn't hurt her. He would just take her for a short ride and then bring her right back to school. That's all. Honest to God, that's all he'd do. No way would he do something that would put him back in prison for another three years! He smiled at Ann. "I bet you'd like to see your dad right now, wouldn't you?"

Ann nodded. She hadn't seen him for a week. She caught at the string at the bottom of her jacket and twisted it around her finger. "Mom says I won't see Dad until April the eighth. He's going to pick me up from school and take me to his place during spring vacation."

Sam rubbed his hands down his jeans. "Your dad said I could take you to him right now. He wants to see you. He said I could drive you and he'd make sure I brought you back in time for classes. Shall we get in my car and go now?"

Ann hesitated. Mom had told her lots of times never to ride with a stranger, but this man really and truly wasn't a stranger. He knew Dad. She looked toward the school and then up at the man.

He held his breath. His heart hammered so loud that he thought she could hear it over the shouts of the kids at the school building. "Shall we go, Ann?"

She barely nodded. He turned to his car and opened the passenger door. His hand shook and he couldn't trust his voice to say anything to her.

She sat on the bucket seat and watched him run around the front of the car. Just as he slid behind the steering wheel she decided she'd better not go with him even if he knew Dad. "I gotta go," she said breathlessly as she pushed on the door handle.

He grabbed her thin arm and jerked her against the gear shift between the seats. She stared at him, her eyes wide with sudden fear. "I can't let you go, Ann!" He knew he sounded desperate. He cleared his throat and whispered, "Just relax and go for a short ride with me. I'll bring you right back."

The color drained from her face and she shook her head.

"Please, Ann."

She opened her mouth to scream. He clamped his hand over it and looked around quickly to see if anyone was watching. He couldn't tell, but no one came to see what was happening and he breathed easier. "Please, Ann, please be quiet and go with me. I'll just take you for a short ride and bring you right back. Honest."

She struggled, but he was too strong for her. She could smell his sweat and the funny odor of his hand. Shivers ran up and down her spine and a bitter taste filled her mouth. Was she being kidnapped the way she'd seen on TV? Did the man really know Dad?

His brain whirled as he tried to decide what to do.

Why wouldn't she just be quiet and go with him? He wasn't a bad person and she should realize that. "Be quiet, Ann!" She struggled harder. "I mean it!" He couldn't sit here and hold her down all morning. He had to get away before someone walked up and asked what was going on.

He bit the inside of his bottom lip. He didn't want to, but he would have to hit her. With the side of his hand he hit her a short, hard chop at the base of her neck. She slumped limply against him.

"That's better." He nodded. "I told you to be quiet, didn't I? I warned you. It's not my fault I had to hit you."

He eased her back in the seat, strapped the seat belt around her, started the car and drove slowly away from the school. Sweat soaked his body. He turned down one side street then another. Gradually his heart slowed until it beat normally. He leaned back and sighed, then smiled down at the little slumped figure beside him. The smell of her clean hair filled his nostrils and he breathed deeply. "Oh, little Annie, you are so beautiful! I'm going to give you a nice ride. I might even take you to Freburg and show you my apartment. Would you like that, Ann? It's not much, but it is mine. I know you'll like it."

He drove past the Bradsville city limit sign and headed toward Freburg. He nodded. "I'll show you my apartment. We'll sit at my little round table and drink Cokes. I might tell you about myself. Would you like that?"

A blue pickup passed him and he slowed a little to let it cut safely in front of him. Trees lined the two-lane highway. Houses nestled among the trees. A police car pulled out of a driveway and turned toward Bradsville. Sam's body prickled with sudden fear. He peeked at Ann then stared straight ahead, his knuckles white from gripping the wheel.

"I don't need to worry. That cop doesn't know what I've done." Sam shrugged. "I didn't do anything wrong. I'm taking Ann for a ride because she misses her dad. They ought to be glad that I care enough to do that for a little girl I saw for the first time only three weeks ago."

He smiled as he remembered. He had stopped at the grocery store in Bradsville and she walked in with a teenage girl. She laughed and chattered and he wanted to speak to her but didn't. Later he followed her home. Since then he had watched her every day as she walked to school with the teenage girl. He frowned. Why hadn't Ann walked with the teenager today?

"Another good omen. Yes, sir, my luck is changing." He nodded. Ann was sitting right here beside him and he was taking her to his place. She would like his place.

Ann moaned and he reached over and gently touched her shoulder.

"I'm glad you're waking up, Ann. I'd hate for you to miss the ride. You should see the countryside all fresh and green with spring. We'll be driving into Freburg soon. Have you been to Freburg before? It's a lot bigger than your little town. We won't be bothered with nosy people like in your town. We'll have fun sitting at my table and talking and drinking Cokes. We can keep each other company."

Suddenly he knew that he would never take her home. He couldn't. She was too important to him. He wouldn't hurt her the way he had the other girls. He frowned and let up on the accelerator. He wouldn't think about the other girls. They had brought too much pain and sorrow into his life. Ann would bring only love and happiness and an end to his loneliness.

Slowly Ann opened her eyes. She saw the man and she heard his voice, but it seemed like a strange dream. A scream rose in her throat and she opened her mouth to let it out, but no sound could pass through the tightness in her throat. He smiled at her and her stomach cramped painfully. He was about Dad's age, but didn't have muscles like Dad. He probably didn't even know Dad.

"You'll like my place, Ann," Sam said cheerfully. "I'll treat you like a little princess. Momma used to treat my sisters like little princesses." He scowled and shoved the thought away. He would not think about his past or he might start to cry. He sometimes did that when he was all alone, but now Ann was here and he couldn't cry in front of her.

"I want to go home," she said in a tiny, scared voice. "Take me home. Please. Please!"

"I will. I promise. But first I want you to see my place." He winked at her, then watched the highway again. He just might take her home in a week or two. He might. "I've only lived there two weeks now. I have a job, you know. I work at Burger King in the kitchen. I make the fries. I'll bring some home for you tomorrow. I don't work today. Thirty hours a week is what I get. It barely pays my rent and my car payment, but I got a good deal on this Chevy. It looks pretty new but it's ten years old. That's pretty good considering Michigan winters with salt and all. Rust, you know. Rusts out fast. My first car rusted out so bad I had to junk it. That was some car." He smiled thinking about it. "I shared it with another guy and we both made payments." He glanced at Ann. "You want to drive a car?"

Tears slipped down her ashen cheeks and she

plucked at the seat belt. Why was he doing this? Why wouldn't he take her back to school? Classes were already started and Miss Foley had marked her absent for the day. "I want to go home."

"Don't keep saying that, Ann. I want you to be happy with me." He stopped at a red traffic signal. A car honked. Traffic was heavy. He spotted two police cars. He sat very still. Finally they drove through the green light and he relaxed.

A few minutes later he turned down Pine Street. "My place is another four blocks. I found it in the want ads and I drove over here and looked at it and I knew it was just the right place. Nothing grand, you know. But it's home."

She brushed away her tears. If she jumped from the car she would get hurt and he'd catch her. Maybe she could roll down the window and shout for help.

"Here we are," he said. He pulled up to a run-down brown duplex. One tiny, bare tree stood in the front yard and a small cedar stood at the side of the house. Bare ground covered most of the yard. Garbage stood piled near the side entrance. "I wish I could've fixed it up a little, but I didn't think I'd bring you here today." Excitement bubbled inside him and he laughed. This really was his lucky day.

A siren wailed and a dog barked from the house just to the right of the duplex.

Sam opened his door and cool air pushed into the car. He ran around and opened her door and unlocked her seat belt. She felt soft and warm. She trembled. How he wanted to pull her close, but he wouldn't make that mistake again. No, he sure wouldn't.

He stepped back and she slowly slipped to the ground and stood before him, shivering with fear.

He unlocked the house and pushed the door open for her to enter first. The smell of burned toast hung in the air.

She stepped inside, shivering so hard she almost fell.

He closed the door and locked it with a sharp click. He smiled at her. "Do you want a Coke? I have milk if you'd like that."

Tears streamed down her cheeks. Her shoulders shook and low whimpering sounds pushed through her tight throat. Why wouldn't he take her back?

Sam opened the small refrigerator and lifted out a liter of Coke. He took two glasses from the cupboard and dropped ice cubes into them. The ice clinked against the glasses and sounded loud in the quiet kitchen. He poured in the Coke and it foamed up to the rim of the glasses and almost over. Pushing aside dirty dishes on the small round table, he set the glasses down and pulled out a chair. "Here, Annie. Sit here. Do you like to be called Annie? I think it's a pretty name. I went to school with a girl named Anne, but she wouldn't let anyone call her Annie. She didn't like me much at all."

Ann felt rooted to the faded linoleum.

Sam gently clasped her arm. She whimpered and sagged away from him but his grip tightened and he forced her to the chair. She sank down with her hands hanging limply at her sides. Gently he wiped her tears with a Burger King napkin. Fresh tears spilled down her face and he wiped them. Finally he gave up and sat down beside her. He sipped his Coke. "Isn't this nice? I've thought about you sitting here with me, talking to me and laughing at my jokes. I could tell you a joke right now if you want me to." He laughed and nodded. "There was a carrot and a lettuce walking down the road. A carrot and a lettuce, see? A truck came along and hit the lettuce. No, it was the carrot." He scratched his head. "There was this truck that came along and hit the carrot, and the lettuce rushed the carrot to the hospital. The doctor took care of the carrot and then walked to the waiting room and said to the lettuce, 'I got good news and bad news. The good news is he'll live. The bad news is he'll be a vegetable all his life.' Get it? A vegetable all his life?" He threw back his head, slapped his thin leg and laughed. She didn't join in and the laugh died in his throat. "Maybe it's above your head. I used to tell my sisters jokes and they never understood them or laughed. I wanted them to, but they never did. My sisters didn't."

Anger rose inside him and he downed the Coke in one gulp, then shoved away from the table and jumped to his feet. He stood at the window, his fists clenched at his sides, his face brick red. He breathed deeply until he felt the anger slip away. Slowly he turned back to Ann. "Drink your Coke. Or do you want milk?"

Chapter 2

Leta Hewitt rang up the sale and pushed the jeans, belt, shirt and sales receipt into the large Gloria's bag. "Thank you. Come again soon."

The woman nodded and hurried away.

Customers browsed through the department store while soft music played in the background. Leta helped a man find a blouse for his wife. The smell of his aftershave turned her stomach. He walked away without the blouse. Leta sighed. Her feet ached inside her black heels and it wasn't even ten in the morning. Maybe she should run home and change shoes. That might help. She shook her head. How she hated going home knowing that it would be empty, empty without a chance of Morgan returning except when he came to pick up Ann.

"Telephone, Leta."

She turned with a frown. Mrs. Briggs hated personal calls coming in for any employee. "I can't imagine who it would be," she said as she walked toward Mrs. Briggs. Ann would be in school and Morgan certainly wouldn't call. He was glad to be away from her. He had repeated it often since their separation. Tears stung her eyes and she quickly blinked them away.

In the small, cluttered office that smelled of coffee and new clothing she picked up the phone, flipped back her shoulder length honey brown hair and said, "Hello."

"This is Jason Grabel, Mrs. Hewitt. From Bradsville Elementary."

Leta sagged against the desk and gripped the receiver tightly. The school had never called her at work even though they had the number in case of an emergency. "Is something wrong with Ann?" she asked sharply.

"That's what I'm trying to find out. Ann isn't in school today."

"What?" Leta's mouth suddenly felt dry. "What did you say? Of course she's in school! Sally walked her to school the same as always!"

"Sally?"

"The babysitter. Sally Perrin. She lives a block from us and she takes care of Ann until I get home from work. She walks Ann to school each morning."

"Ann's not here, Mrs. Hewitt."

The room seemed to spin wildly as Leta leaped up. "Then where is she? Where?" Her voice rose and she knew anyone standing outside the office could hear. "Tell me where she is!"

"She is not in school and that's all we know."

"Is that how you take care of the children entrusted to you?" The pink collar on her blouse felt too tight and her light wool jacket and skirt too hot.

"Calm down, Mrs. Hewitt."

"Calm down? Calm down, you say?" Leta paced as far as the phone cord would allow. "How can you suggest that to me? I am her mother! And you tell me she's missing!"

"I didn't really say 'missing'."

"I'll be right there and you'd better have an explanation for this." She slammed down the receiver and ran from the office. "Mrs. Briggs, I must leave!"

Several customers stared at her, but she was past caring about appearances.

Mrs. Briggs caught Leta's arm. "What's wrong, Leta?"

"Ann is missing." Leta grabbed her purse and ran for the door, rummaging for her keys with a trembling hand. Ann couldn't really be missing. Could she? This was just another nightmare like the ones she'd been having since Morgan walked out.

In the parking lot she dropped her keys beside the car. With tears stinging her eyes she bent to pick them up and the contents spilled from her purse. Groaning in frustration she scooped up makeup, wallet, and a pen that Morgan had given her last month. "Please, God. Please let her be all right."

At the school she ran across the grass to the front door. Cool wind whipped her hair back and brought color to her cheeks. Her blue eyes were wide with fear. She flung open the door and ran inside, her heels clicking loudly on the tile floor. She smelled popcorn and coffee and heard children laughing as she rushed toward the third grade room.

A hand grabbed her arm and she gasped and stopped.

"She's not in her classroom, Mrs. Hewitt," said Jason Grabel softly. "Come to my office. We don't want to disturb the other students, do we? It's better if we sit quietly and talk. It's too early to panic, I'm sure."

She shivered, clutched her purse tightly and walked beside him to his office. "My baby. What happened to my precious baby?" she whispered hoarsely.

In the office he held a chair for her while she sank down gratefully. He leaned against the desk. Mr. Grabel rubbed his round, red cheek and cleared his throat. He understood her panic but he couldn't allow the entire school to become terrified. It was hard enough to handle just one frightened parent. His gray suit coat swung open to show his crisp white shirt, red and gray tie and gray pants. "Try to calm down a little, Mrs. Hewitt, and let's talk. Is there anywhere Ann could have gone? Grandparents? Friends?"

"No! I don't know!" At one time she could say for sure what Ann would or would not do but, since the separation, Ann had been unpredictable.

"Would she run away from home?" He hated suggesting it, but he had to.

Leta rocked back and forth, clutching her purse protectively to her. "I don't know. I don't know!" Would she? "No. No! She wouldn't run away."

"Could she be with your husband?"

"Yes! Maybe." She jumped up. "I'll call Morgan. Maybe she's with him. Maybe she is." She scooped up the white phone and pressed the numbers in short jerky movements. Just as the phone rang she remembered she'd dialed her home number. She slammed down the receiver and clung to the side of the desk, her head spinning.

"Would you like me to dial?"

She nodded. "Do you have his office number?"

"Yes. I would have called him sooner, but you did ask me to always contact you and not him." Jason Grabel flipped through the Rolodex and found the number of Queen Manufacturing. His hand shook as he reached for the phone. He frowned in irritation. Surely he could handle an emergency better than this. But this was a new experience for him. He hoped it would not get worse. He couldn't fall apart in front of the parent. He jabbed the numbers and listened to it ring. His voice broke as he asked for

Morgan Hewitt. He glanced at Leta Hewitt as she slumped in the chair. "They're getting him."

She nodded and pressed a tissue to her eyes.

Morgan picked up the phone at his desk and frowned. He'd been called away from a couple of workers who had been giving him trouble on the line the past two days and he didn't have time for a phone call. The sleeves of his white shirt were rolled up to his forearm showing the dark hairs on his arms. His black dress pants fit snugly around his narrow hips without being tight. "Hello," he said sharply.

"Mr. Hewitt, this is Jason Grabel from Ann's school."

Morgan frowned. "Yes?"

"Is Ann with you?"

"No. She's in school. Isn't she?"

"Could you come to the school immediately?"

The color drained from his face. "Has Ann been hurt on the playground? Did you call her mother?"

"Please come. Mrs. Hewitt is here with me. She asked me to call you. Ann didn't come to school today."

Morgan dropped the receiver with a clatter, grabbed his jacket from his chair and ran through the noisy plant to his car. At the gate he shouted to the security guard, "Tell Miles I had a family emergency and that he'll have to get someone to cover for me."

A few minutes later he roared out of the parking lot, his knuckles white from gripping the steering wheel. "Heavenly Father, take care of Ann. Don't let anything bad happen to her. And help me to keep my temper with Leta so we can handle whatever it is."

He thumped the steering wheel. Why had he left Leta and Ann? He should have stayed no matter how hard it was to get along with Leta. Or he should have taken Ann with him.

At the school he screeched to a stop behind Leta's gold Honda Civic. His heart hammered painfully in his chest as he ran toward the door. Cool spring wind ruffled his brown hair. Children swarmed across the back playground, shouting and laughing. He burst through the doors and ran toward the office, his face pale and his hazel eyes full of anguish. The knot in his stomach tightened as he pushed open the office door. He saw Leta huddled in a yellow chair, her makeup smeared and Jason Grabel leaning back against his desk as if he didn't know what to do.

"Just what's going on?" Morgan's voice was gruff and the words hurt his throat.

Leta sprang toward him. Instinctively he stepped back. Leta froze in place. "Ann's ... not here," she said.

"What do you mean, not here?" Morgan looked helplessly from Leta to Jason Grabel. "Where is she?"

"We hoped you'd know." Jason Grabel cleared his throat. "Have you seen her?"

Leta swayed and reluctantly Morgan steadied her with a strong arm around her narrow waist. His touch stopped her trembling. Seeing her so out of control frightened him more than hearing that Ann wasn't in school.

"What about the girl who walks her to school every morning?" asked Morgan around a lump in his throat. "Have you called Sally?"

Leta shook her head.

"I'll call her!" Morgan eased Leta to the chair and grabbed the phone, then stopped. "What's the number of the high school?"

Jason Grabel told him and Morgan jabbed the numbers. When a woman answered he barked,

"This is an emergency. I must speak to Sally Perrin immediately."

"Who's calling?"

A muscle jumped in Morgan's jaw. "Morgan Hewitt. Sally's my little girl's babysitter."

"Just a moment, Mr. Hewitt."

Morgan tapped his toe and waited.

"What?" asked Leta, plucking at his sleeve.

"They're getting Sally," he said.

The woman on the other end said, "I'm sorry, but Sally is absent today. Her mother called in this morning and said she was sick."

Morgan dropped the receiver and faced Leta, accusingly. "Sally is home sick! She let Ann walk on her own!"

"No. No, Sally wouldn't do that! I can count on Sally."

"What's her home number?" asked Morgan grimly.

Leta told him and he dialed quickly. Deb Perrin answered. "This is Morgan Hewitt, Deb. May I speak with Sally? It's an emergency."

"Sally's in school."

"No. We just called the school and they said she's out sick. She was supposed to walk Ann to school."

"She did. She always does."

Leta grabbed the phone. "Deb, Ann is missing and so is Sally if she's not at home. We'll be right over."

"But I'm leaving this minute for Detroit."

"You wait for us!" Leta dropped the receiver and ran for the door.

Outdoors Morgan caught her hand and led her to his car. She sank back on the seat, shivering as she gripped her purse with both hands.

He started the car and turned on the heat to stop her shivering. "There has to be a reasonable explanation for this, Leta."

"Does there?" she asked bitterly.

"God is our strength."

Leta bit back a sharp answer. She didn't believe in God the way she used to, but right now she didn't want to get into it with Morgan.

At Perrin's driveway Morgan slammed on the brakes and blocked Deb from backing out. She slipped out of her car and stood beside it, her face red with anger.

Leta ran to Deb. "Ann is gone and I must talk to Sally!"

"Is she in the house?" asked Morgan, heading toward the side door.

"She's not there! I told you that!" Deb shrugged. "She probably skipped school to go shopping. Maybe she took Ann with her. Relax, will you? In a few hours they'll be home where they belong and you'll laugh about the whole thing."

Morgan stabbed his fingers through his hair. He wanted to shake the woman and make her see the seriousness of the situation. "Deb, where does Sally usually shop?"

"Downtown unless she catches a ride to Freburg."

Leta bit her lip and groaned. Deb had never kept a close eye on Sally. "Who are Sally's friends? Who would know where she is today?"

Deb frowned. "Phyllis Cooley. Gina Trumbell. I guess I could call the school and see if they know anything. But maybe they went with Sally and Ann."

"Call them," snapped Morgan.

Deb suddenly felt the extreme tension in the air and it sent a shiver of fear over her. She grabbed her purse from the front seat of her car, pushed the car door shut with her hip and ran to the door as she searched for the house key.

Several minutes later Deb turned to Leta and

Morgan. "Gina said Sally went to Freburg with Phyllis. She said Ann told Sally she could walk to school alone." Deb's voice faded away and she sank to a kitchen chair as she watched the look of horror cross Leta's face.

"She *is* missing," whispered Leta, swaying against Morgan. "What're we going to do?"

Deb studied the tidy kitchen. It smelled of cinnamon and coffee. The sun brightened the yellow curtains and warmed the room. A clock ticked in the hall near the front door. She jumped up. She had to get going.

"We'd better call the police," said Morgan hoarsely.

Leta shook her head. "First we'll call our parents."

"We'll go see them instead," said Morgan. He turned to Deb. "Tell Sally we want to talk to her the minute she gets home."

Deb nodded.

In the car Morgan whispered, "We'll find her, Leta." He hated to see her so torn up. "We'll find her and bring her home where she belongs." The words sounded hollow to him and he closed his mouth and bit back a moan.

Leta glanced at him, then quickly looked away, her hands locked in her lap.

He drove a few blocks in painful silence. "She could've gone to visit Burl and Wanda."

"Mom would call me at work," said Leta stiffly. "You know that."

Scowling, Morgan pressed his foot to the accelerator and gripped the steering wheel tighter.

Chapter 3

Wanda Stanley leaned against the counter and poured her third cup of coffee that morning. The back door slammed and she jerked around with a frown. She glanced down at her old floor-length dressing gown and matching blue slippers. Why hadn't she dressed earlier instead of watching TV?

Burl walked in, rubbing his hand over his balding head. He looked her up and down. "Still not dressed, Wanda?"

"I didn't feel like it. What does it matter? I have nowhere to go today." She opened the cupboard door and lifted down his favorite mug. She held it up, her fine brow raised questioningly.

He nodded as he sat at the maple table. "A cup might perk me up." He had managed Clawson's Grocery for the past twenty-four years. Lately it had really been getting to him, but he pushed the feelings of anger and frustration away and just kept working. What else could he do? He and Wanda were too old to change their way of life just so he could do something interesting and challenging. He looked up as Wanda set the cup of steaming coffee in front of him. "Did you talk to Leta this morning?"

Wanda sank to her chair. "For a few minutes." She moved the flowered centerpiece to the side so she could see Burl. "Leta said she was running a little late, so she couldn't stay on the phone long."

Burl sipped his coffee, rubbed his hand across his bushy mustache and sighed. "Our daughter made one mistake in her life and that was marrying Morgan Hewitt."

Wanda locked her hands together in her lap. She really was tired of hearing Burl say that but, since the separation, she agreed with him. Morgan really wasn't the right man for Leta. "I suppose the whole marriage was a mistake. Except for our darling Ann." Wanda smiled as she studied the picture on the refrigerator that Ann had colored two days ago when she spent the night. "Ann might be here for supper tonight. And for the night if Leta agrees."

"I'll make sure I get home in time to see Ann. We'll have fun on the computer again. She's getting good with a couple of the games." Burl shook his head. "And she's only nine. When I was nine I couldn't even add. She's a bright girl. Takes after our side of the family, that's for sure." He stood up, pulled off his dark blue suit coat and hung it over the back of his chair.

Wanda watched him pull out a pack of doughnuts from the bread drawer. He really was too thin and his nose was much too large for his narrow face. He stood a good head taller than she. His hair was already gray. She kept hers brown, a little lighter shade than before it had turned gray. She smoothed her blue robe over her slender legs. "Ann and Leta are going to church with us Sunday. I was surprised Leta agreed."

Burl scowled and his bushy brows touched over his nose. "That church they go to is too fanatical. I told Leta when Morgan first went overboard with religion that she was making a mistake. I'm glad she sees how wrong she was. I'd hate to see Ann ruin her life with too much religion."

Wanda sighed. "Morgan and Leta seemed too religious to let their marriage end in divorce."

Just then the back door slammed and Wanda jumped to her feet, holding her robe tightly around her. "Who in the world could it be?" Greg and Evan lived too far away to drop in. Leta was at work and Ann in school.

Burl slipped into his jacket. He hated to be seen in shirt sleeves.

Leta burst into the kitchen with Morgan on her heels. Wildly she looked around the room. "Is Ann here?"

"Ann?" Wanda reached for Leta. "My dear, what's wrong?"

"What's wrong?" repeated Burl in alarm.

"Ann's gone," said Morgan.

Leta burst into tears again. Morgan reached for her, but she shrugged him away and flung herself into Burl's arms.

Morgan rammed his fists into his pockets and looked away.

"Daddy, Ann is gone and we can't find her!"

Burl looked down at Leta, then hesitantly wrapped his long arms around her. "Did you say she's gone?"

Wanda inched to her chair and sat down, her brown eyes wide with alarm as she searched Morgan's face. "Tell us," she whispered.

Morgan rubbed an unsteady hand across his eyes. He hated coming here where he wasn't welcome. His voice cracked as he explained what they'd learned. "We thought she might be here."

"She's not!" snapped Burl. "Have you reported it to the police?"

Leta pulled away and dabbed at her tears with a napkin from the table. "Is that necessary?"

"We wanted to make sure she wasn't here or with my folks," said Morgan.

"Maybe she's hiding because we hurt her." Leta rubbed her jacket. She couldn't look at Morgan. "She'd be so embarrassed if we sent the police out looking for her."

"She would," said Wanda.

"We're going to see my folks now," said Morgan. He looked hesitantly at Leta. "Unless you want to stay here."

"Oh, do!" cried Wanda.

"Stay with us," said Burl. "You can rest here. Morgan can call if he learns anything."

Leta hesitated. It would be wonderful to be protected and pampered again. She glanced at Morgan. The agony on his face touched her heart. It was past time to be pampered and protected. She stepped toward Morgan and blindly reached out to him. "I want to stay with you and find Ann."

He caught her icy hand in his and clung tightly to it, then ran with her to his car. He was glad she'd stayed with him.

Wanda sat very still and listened for the car to drive away. The roar faded in the distance and scalding tears slipped down her face.

Burl slumped to his chair, suddenly looking very old and very tired. "What is this world coming to? Little girls aren't safe to walk to school." He slammed his left fist into his right palm with a loud smack and Wanda jumped. "I'd like to tell that babysitter a thing or two! How dare she leave that little baby to walk to school alone?"

Wanda pressed her hands to her face and her slender shoulders shook with great racking sobs. She didn't often cry. She tried to gulp back the tears, but they kept coming. Her head whirled. She wanted to cry out to God but didn't know how to talk to Him. He was not personal to her the way He was to Leta and Morgan. Now that she had a need large enough to take to God, she didn't know how. Her sobs grew louder and wilder.

Burl listened to her and trembled. He'd never seen her lose control. What should he do? Unexpected tears filled his eyes and he blinked them away. He glanced at the clock. It was time to go back to work. He tried to stand but his legs felt too weak. He reached across to Wanda and awkwardly patted her shoulder. "Sh-sh-sh. Don't cry."

She lifted her tear-stained face. "Hold me, Burl. Help me."

Slowly he walked to her side and awkwardly lifted her in his arms. She clung to him and he wrapped his arms around her. She sobbed against his shoulder and he stared out the wide window in back of the maple table. He saw two cars pass. Birds flew around the bushes. The only sound he heard was Wanda's sobs. He had held her to kiss her or to make love, but he had never held her to comfort her before. He moved restlessly, unsure of what to do next. He said gruffly, "It's that Morgan Hewitt's fault! He should never have walked out on our little girl and her baby. If he made enough money so Leta wouldn't need to work, then she would've been home to take care of Ann. It's Morgan's fault all right and I'll tell him the first chance I get!"

Burl dropped his arms from Wanda. She stood stiffly with her arms around him. Finally she stepped back and he felt better.

"I don't want anything to happen to Ann," whispered Wanda. "I couldn't live if anything happened to her. Please don't fight with Morgan now. We have to work together to get our baby back."

"Sure, sure." He wouldn't argue with her when she was in this mood, but when he was alone with Morgan he'd have his say. "Go wash your face, Wanda. Get dressed and put on your makeup. You look terrible. I have to get back to work."

Her face crumpled. "Don't leave me alone now. I can't be alone."

"I have to go to work. You know that." He turned away from her. He hated to see her look so old and ugly with a runny nose and red eyes. "Pull yourself together."

She ducked her head and twisted the ties of her robe. Why should she expect him to comfort her? He had never been able to do that, not even when she miscarried their last baby, a baby girl who would be nineteen years old tomorrow if she'd lived. Girls were so special. Not that she didn't love Evan and Greg, but they had been rowdy and hard to raise, not easy and fun like Leta had been, like the baby would've been. Secretly, in her own mind, she'd named the baby Ann. When Leta and Morgan had named their baby girl Ann, she showered all her pent-up love on their Ann.

Ann could not be missing! What if they never found her? Many missing children were never recovered.

Wanda touched Ann's drawing on the refrigerator. In her mind she heard Ann's laughter and chatter.

"I am leaving now," said Burl as he hesitated by the kitchen door. "I'll be back for supper. Call me if you hear anything." He waited but she didn't turn or speak and finally he walked into the cool April sunshine to his car. How glad he was that he had a job to attend! If he had to stay home and do nothing he'd go crazy. At work he could keep busy. Then he wouldn't think about Ann or about Wanda's need for comfort.

Wanda heard the car pull away and slowly walked to the immaculate living room. She turned on her soap opera to let the words fill the quiet house. From the coffee table she picked up the photo album of Ann and sank to the dusty-rose, crushed velvet sofa.

Gently Wanda stroked the picture of Ann taken when she was a day old in the hospital. "My Ann would've looked just like you, Ann Louise. The little scrunched-up face, round rose and slits for eyes. And she would've turned into the beauty that you did."

Wanda touched the next photo of Ann taken when she was three months old. "Nothing must happen to you, Ann. You will stay alive and you will grow up. You'll have fun being a teenager. When you're old enough you'll fall in love and get married. I'll help you buy your wedding gown like I did your mother. You'll marry a fine young man, a man who loves you and will comfort you when you're sad or lonely or hurt."

Wanda's voice broke and she sank back, closed her eyes and let the blare of the TV fill the silence of the house and her life.

Chapter 4

Dolly Hewitt clicked off the vacuum cleaner and stood in the middle of her living room, her head cocked and her green eyes narrowed thoughtfully. Something was wrong. She could feel it. "John? Is it John, Father God?" John was out finishing the chores. Soon he'd be in for lunch. The aroma of chicken noodle soup and fresh biscuits filled the air. She had also tossed a salad and baked an apple pie.

"Keep John safe from all harm, Heavenly Father," she prayed as she clicked on the appliance again. As she pushed the sweeper back and forth over the rust-colored carpet she prayed for her four children, eight grandchildren, then the church and Pastor Ogden. The uneasy feeling pressed heavier on her. She continued to pray as she put the vacuum cleaner back in the closet, then walked to the kitchen. She stopped short when she saw John dishing up the soup. "You're in early," she said.

"I thought I heard you call me." John studied her with thoughtful brown eyes. He had gray hair and wore faded jeans and a blue plaid work shirt. He was still as strong and muscular as when she first married him.

"I didn't call." She tugged her blue sweater down over her jeans as she walked to the sink to wash her hands. Warm water ran over her hands and wrists.

She glanced over her shoulder. "Something's wrong, John. I can feel it."

He carried the basket of biscuits to the table. "Let's pray," he said softly.

She held out her hands and he took them in his work-roughened ones. They bowed their heads and he prayed for the people she had prayed for earlier.

"And Father, thank you for the food. It's blessed in Jesus' name. Amen." John pulled her close and kissed her.

Dolly kissed him back the way she had for the past thirty-five years. "That's the best part of the meal," she said.

He nodded. "Did you hear from Morgan today?"

"Not today. Yesterday I talked to him. He's in such agony over leaving Leta and Ann."

John buttered a hot biscuit. "Satan has Morgan blinded right now, but Satan is defeated! That family belongs to God and He'll help bring them together again."

"That's right." Dolly nodded as she dipped her spoon in the thick noodles with large chunks of chicken.

Outdoors the dog barked.

"Someone's coming," said John.

"Maybe it's the mailman," said Dolly.

"No. Granger barks different for the mailman." John pushed back his chair and strode to the door. He opened it to find Morgan and Leta running up the walk from their car.

"Oh, my!" said Dolly, jumping up.

John's stomach knotted painfully when he saw the look on Morgan's face. "What's wrong?"

"Ann!" said Morgan.

"Is she here?" asked Leta.

"She's not here," said Dolly. "We talked to her last

night, but she's not here. Why would she be?"

Morgan paced the kitchen as he told what had happened. Leta added a detail here and there in a hysterical voice.

John pulled Morgan close with one arm and Leta with the other. "Let's pray," he said. He waited until Dolly completed the circle.

Leta sighed and closed her eyes. She knew John and Dolly's prayers were answered.

Morgan leaned against the strength he felt from his dad and closed his eyes. In the past several months he had stopped praying.

"Heavenly Father, in Jesus' name we bind the evil spirits that are trying to harm Ann. We send angels to guard her and keep her safe. Help us to find her and bring her home safely. Send the right people to help us. Comfort Ann wherever she is and help her remember that You are with her. Comfort Morgan and Leta so they can calmly search for Ann and find her. Show us what to do and where to go. Thank You, Father. In Jesus' name we pray. Amen."

Tears welled up in Dolly's eyes and slipped down her cheeks. She hugged Leta. "Don't give up, honey. Never, never give up. You'll get her back."

Leta stiffened and pulled away. It was hard to be around Morgan's parents. They always made her feel so cold toward God.

"Thanks, Dad," whispered Morgan as he hugged John, then Dolly. "Thanks, Mom."

"What'll you do now?" asked Dolly.

"Talk to Ann's teachers, the students, our neighbors."

"Let us know when you hear anything," said John.

"We'll keep in touch," said Morgan.

"We'll continue to intercede," said Dolly.

Morgan kissed his mother and hugged his dad,

then walked out with Leta, his heart a little lighter and the black cloud lifted.

Dolly walked into John's arms and wrapped her arms around his waist with her cheek pressed against his. She felt his heart thudding against her. "Oh, John!"

"Our little Ann," he whispered hoarsely. "Nothing must happen to her." He lifted his head and his brown eyes flashed. "And nothing will! Satan is not going to have a victory! We won't let him!"

"I'll call Pastor Ogden and tell him. Then I'll ask Denise to send it around on the women's prayer chain," said Dolly. "There's not much we can do in the natural, but in the spiritual realm we'll fight this battle and win!" Dolly's voice broke and she rubbed her hand across her nose. Her hand shook slightly as she dialed Ogden's number.

John paced the floor, praying under his breath, his fists doubled at his sides. A rooster crowed outdoors and the dog barked at it. Water dripped in the sink and he stopped and closed the faucet tightly. He walked to Dolly and stood with his arm around her shoulder as she talked on the phone to Ben Ogden. She leaned against John, thankful that he was always there for her.

Ben Ogden finally hung up, turned from the phone and reached for Denise. "The little Hewitt girl is missing."

"Ann?"

"Yes." Ben's stomach cramped and he held Denise tighter. Kennie and Heidi were Ann's age and he'd go wild if anything happened to them. "I told Dolly that you'd call the prayer chain," he said after he told her the story.

"Every time I think that nothing worse can happen, I'm surprised to hear it can," she whispered as she dabbed away her tears. "We must visit Morgan and Leta and help them all we can."

"If they'll let us," said Ben. In the past eight years of pastoring, he had helped several people in bad situations, often without telling Denise. She became too upset when she heard about the sufferings of others. He was glad for her compassion, but he didn't like to see her hurt. He touched her auburn hair as she reached for the phone to call the first person on the prayer chain.

He glanced at his watch, suddenly anxious for Kennie and Heidi to get home from school.

Denise hung up the phone and turned back to Ben. "I know something happened that made Leta pull away from God. I wonder what. One time she almost opened up to me, then she froze and wouldn't let me get close again. When she comes to church now she avoids me. I think she's afraid she will break down and confide in me."

Ben nodded. "I don't know what caused the change in her. Morgan hasn't been the same either. But we'll continue to pray." He rubbed his finger down the side of her face and kissed her. They clung together and prayed for Ann and for their own children.

Inside the city limits Morgan slowed the car to thirty-five miles per hour. He glanced at Leta. She hadn't said a word since they left his parents, but he could feel her tension. He knew that she was very uncomfortable around his family since the separation.

Leta moaned and leaned her head back against the seat, suddenly feeling faint.

A few minutes later they stood in Marilyn Foley's class. Marilyn stood at the back of the room listening to them. She was sorry to learn that Ann was missing, but surely it was too soon for Mrs. Hewitt to be so upset. Ann had not been herself lately. She could have gone to the park for the day.

Glenna Richards held up her hand, then waved it for more attention as the Hewitts continued to talk. Marilyn frowned and shook her head, but Glenna waved harder.

"I'm sorry, Mr. Hewitt," said Marilyn. He was nice looking and she wanted to impress him. She knew she looked pretty in her red dress. She certainly was more attractive than Mrs. Hewitt. He deserved better. "What is it, Glenna?"

"I think I saw Ann talking to a man this morning before the school doors were open." Glenna felt very important saying it. She wanted to add more but didn't know what else to say.

Leta stepped toward Glenna. "Did you see what the man looked like?"

"He was just a man."

"Exactly where were they when you saw them?" asked Morgan.

Glenna screwed up her face. "Right out there." She pointed toward the front of the school. "I think."

Leta frowned. "Was she talking to a man or not?"

Glenna sank low in her seat. "I guess she was."

Just then a picture flashed in Marilyn Foley's mind of Ann standing near the curb talking to a man. She sucked in air and pressed her hand to her midriff. Should she speak up now? What would Morgan think of her for forgetting such an important item? Maybe it wasn't significant, but at least she would do her part by saying something. She cleared her throat and waited until Morgan finished questioning Glenna. "I think Glenna did see Ann talking to a man."

Morgan stared at Miss Foley and Leta gasped.

"Why do you say that?" snapped Leta, locking her icy hands together in front of her.

"I looked out the window this morning before school started and I noticed Ann walking alone along the sidewalk. She stopped and talked to a man who got out of a car parked at the curb."

"Why didn't you say something sooner?" cried Leta.

Marilyn shrugged and tried to hide her embarrassment. "I had forgotten about it until Glenna mentioned it. I am sorry."

"What did the man look like?" asked Morgan.

"I didn't know him. I see so many parents that it's really hard to say. But, no, I'm sure I didn't know him."

"What did he look like?" asked Leta around the tight lump in her throat.

Marilyn narrowed her eyes in thought. "Short, slight, mid to late twenties. Maybe thirties. It's so hard to judge age, isn't it? And he had a beard. I think." The picture in her mind was fuzzy and she couldn't remember what he wore or even the color of his hair.

Morgan looked at the class of silent students. "Did any of you see the man she described?"

They shook their heads.

"If you ever see him, tell Miss Foley so she can call us." Morgan turned to the teacher. "If you ever see him, or if you think of anything else, call me. Please. We're going to the other classes now." He caught Leta's hand and walked her out of the room into the quiet hallway.

"She talked to a man," whispered Leta. "How many times have we told her not to talk to strangers?"

"Maybe he wasn't a stranger," said Morgan. A chill ran down his spine. He'd heard of abductions where the abductor turned out to be the mailman, the teacher, or the man next door, not a stranger at all.

"I can't take it, Morgan," Leta whispered as she sagged against him.

"I know, I know." He held her for a moment, then walked to the next classroom with her.

Several minutes later they walked to his car. Two other children had seen Ann talking to the man, but none of the descriptions matched.

"Now what?" asked Leta tiredly as she tucked her honey brown hair behind her ears.

"We wait for Sally to return. She probably won't be back until school's out for the day." He sounded tired even to himself. "I think we both need something to eat."

"I can't eat."

"We have to keep up our strength."

She sighed. "You're right. But I can't go to a restaurant." She touched her puffy eyes.

"We'll get soup and sandwiches. Maybe a cup of tea. I'll take you home."

"Yours or mine?" she asked bitterly.

"Whatever you want," he said stiffly.

She peeked at him through dark lashes. She really wanted to see his place and find out how he lived without her. "Your place," she finally said. Impatiently she turned away and stared out the window as he drove. How could she think if anything but Ann right now?

Several minutes later he stopped outside the house where he lived. Once it had been a grand house. Now it was four apartments, none of them grand. He couldn't afford anything better and still give Leta money each week. "Home sweet home," he muttered as he opened the car door. Cool air rushed in. Music drifted out from Mary Teater's apartment and he frowned. Right now he couldn't take loud music.

Leta stumbled on a crack in the sidewalk and he caught her arm to steady her. She pulled away, suddenly unable to take his touch. "I guess I'm more exhausted than I thought."

"We'll eat and you can rest before we talk to Sally." He unlocked the door, opened it and stood aside for her to enter. His stomach fluttered and he frowned impatiently.

She looked around with interest that turned into admiration. That angered her. She had wanted the room to be dirty and ugly. But it was neat and clean. The plaid sofa looked worn but comfortable. A tiny kitchen stood at one end of the room with an open door at the other end. "You're a good housekeeper. That is, if you've done it yourself."

"I did." He remembered the days at home when she complained about his dirty socks under the bed—the bed they shared. He pushed the thought aside with a flush. "Please sit down while I heat a can of soup."

She followed him to the kitchen and stood beside the small formica table. Sudden tears filled her eyes. "Will she really be all right, Morgan?"

"She has to be," he said hoarsely. "Please, sit down and relax while I make lunch." He saw the tired lines around her eyes and the pinched look at her mouth. "Please, honey, sit down and rest."

She turned away in confusion. He called her 'honey' and he hadn't done that in a very long time. She sank to the chair. His worn Bible lay within reach and she remembered the nights he read to her before they went to bed. She bit her lower lip. "Have you seen a lawyer about a divorce?"

His hand jerked and he almost dropped the tea-kettle. Did she want him to start divorce proceedings? He pushed back the terrible thought. "This is not the time to think about that."

She felt relieved and that surprised her. "I suppose you're right."

He put the water on to boil and opened a can of tomato soup. Loud music from next door filled the room.

Leta pushed herself up and walked restlessly around the room. She stopped at the door and peeked into the bedroom. The bed was well made. A pair of worn sneakers stood at the foot of the bed. A pink shirt was draped over a chair. Was it the pink shirt she bought for his birthday? He had refused to wear it. Maybe he decided it did look handsome on him. The room looked stark and lonely. Abruptly she turned away from it. "Are you comfortable here, Morgan?"

"I suppose so." He didn't tell her how lonely it was at night and how he hated to sit down alone to eat a meal.

She walked back to the table and once again sank to the chair. He set two cups of tea on the table. Tears welled up in her eyes and she blinked them away.

Morgan handed her a cracker with cheddar cheese on it. Reluctantly she took it and nibbled it.

She sipped her tea while he dished up the soup. "Don't give me much," she said.

"I didn't." He set the bowls on the table and sat on the only other chair. He looked at the tomato soup. "I can't eat," he said just above a whisper.

"I know." She pressed her fingers to her temples.

"We'll each eat a bite or two and then go," he said.

She nodded. Slowly she dipped in her spoon and lifted the soup to her lips.

His hand shook as he picked up his spoon.

Chapter 5

Sally Perrin unlocked the Hewitt's back door and stepped into the silent house. She flipped back her blond curls and draped her jean jacket over a kitchen chair. She looked around guiltily. She shouldn't have had Ann walk to school and home alone today. She shrugged. "So? It's too late to think about it now." She opened the refrigerator and pulled out the pitcher of orange juice.

The cold juice tasted good and felt cool in her throat. She rinsed out her glass and loaded it in the dishwasher with the breakfast dishes. With a sigh she leaned against the sink. Shopping hadn't been much fun. It had been great to get away from boring, boring classes. But it wouldn't be easy to make up the classes tomorrow. Algebra and history were so hard.

Slowly she walked to the living room. The one-story house was small: two bedrooms, one bathroom, a study, living room, kitchen with a breakfast nook, and a full basement. Sometimes she pretended it was her house and she and Jim were married and lived in it. She rolled her eyes as she brushed her hand over the TV set. Jim didn't know she existed and she couldn't get up enough nerve to let him know.

She glanced at the clock and frowned. Ann really should be home by now. Maybe she misunderstood and thought she was to meet Sally and walk home together as usual.

Sally picked up Ann's stuffed rabbit and tossed it on the bed. She would wait ten more minutes and if Ann wasn't home then, she'd take the route they always walked and find her. It was no big deal. What could possibly happen in such a dead town? Mrs. Hewitt worried too much, even more since Mr. Hewitt had moved out. Sally wrinkled her nose. She sure would never let a man like Mr. Hewitt go if she was married to him. He was good looking and drove a nice car. "I'd never let him move out and find someone else."

Sally walked back to the kitchen and looked out at the front yard. Nervously she rubbed her hands down her faded jeans and tucked her red shirt in at her narrow waist. Her body was reed-thin and sometimes she worried that she was too skinny.

A dog ran across the grass with one of the neighbor boys in pursuit. Where was Ann? It wasn't like her to take so long to come home. Ann knew that if it wasn't raining they were to walk to her Grandma Stanley's right after school. Sally looked up at the bright blue sky.

"Where are you, Ann?" Sally shivered. Had she made a big mistake by having Ann walk home alone?

This morning she had asked Ann, "Are you sure you can walk to and from school by yourself?"

"Sure I can," Ann said with great confidence.

"You won't be afraid?"

"Why should I be? I'm in third grade. I can walk to school and home by myself. I can!"

"If you're sure."

"I'm sure."

"You know you can't tell your mom. She'd be real mad at me if she found out. She might fire me."

"I won't tell Mom. She'll never, ever find out and

she won't fire you."

With a laugh Sally had hugged Ann. "I'll bring you something from the mall. I promise." She looked toward her purse on the counter. She had found a tiny bear for Ann, one that she could tuck in her pocket and carry to school. It was fuzzy and soft and cute and would go with her bear collection.

Sally walked to Ann's room and looked inside. It smelled of the perfume that Ann spilled several days ago. The bed wasn't made. Sally stood the rabbit on the chair and pulled the sheet and blankets in place. She picked up two bears from the floor and set them on the shelf where Ann usually kept them. She set the panda bear on the bed. Sally touched the clown picture hanging above the toy chest. She looked in the mirror on the closet door, then looked closer. Was she getting a zit on her nose from that greasy stuff she'd eaten today? No, it was only a shadow. She walked to the window and looked out at the small backyard where there was a swing set and a sandbox.

Just then Sally heard the door close and she laughed in relief. She really had been tense. "Ann," she called as she ran to the living room. "Where have you been, Ann?"

She stopped short when she saw Morgan and Leta standing in the kitchen. Both of them looked frightened and then angry. Sally felt her face turn bright red with embarrassment. "I thought you were Ann," she said weakly.

"She's gone," said Leta in a dead voice.

"Missing," said Morgan as he stabbed his fingers through his thick dark hair.

"What?" Sally backed away, her eyes wide in horror.

"Why did you let her walk to school alone?" asked

Leta as she gripped Sally's thin arm. "Why?"

Fear stung Sally's skin and she was too weak to pull away from Leta's painful grip. "I . . . I'm sorry."

Morgan gently pried Leta's fingers from Sally's arm and Sally stumbled back against the wall. The room seemed suddenly too quiet, too full of tension.

"Sit down, Sally," said Morgan coldly. "We want some answers *now*."

Sally walked slowly to the table and perched on the edge of a chair. She watched Leta and Morgan sit side by side across from her. Ann's chair was empty except for Sally's jean jacket.

Morgan cleared his throat. "Ann didn't go to school today. We don't know where she is. Do you know?"

"She promised she'd walk right to school and come right home after," whispered Sally.

"Some of the students saw her talking to a man outside the school," said Leta. "Do you know who it could be?"

Sally shook her head.

Morgan described the man and Sally shook her head again.

"She never talked to strangers before," said Sally weakly. "Why would she today? Oh, I am so sorry that I didn't walk her to school today! *I am so, so sorry!*"

"Not as sorry as we are," snapped Leta. She jumped up, jerked Sally's jacket off Ann's chair and tossed it at her. "Get out of here and never come back. Do you hear me?"

Sally clutched her jacket and the smell of French fries and smoke drifted up from it. She looked wildly at Morgan and Leta, grabbed her purse and ran from their house. They blamed her for Ann being missing. They had every right! It was her fault! All her fault!

She ran all the way home and let herself in the back door. The silence pressed in on her and she wanted to shout for Mom to come and comfort her, but she knew Mom was in Detroit and wouldn't be home until tomorrow. Sally leaned against the door, her chest rising and falling, her breathing ragged.

Mom had said she was going shopping in Detroit, but Sally knew better. Mom had a lover. She was trying to keep it from Dad. He wouldn't care anyway but he might not hand out money so freely if he knew. He wouldn't be home until Sunday afternoon.

With a moan Sally walked to her silent bedroom and flopped face down on the carefully made bed. She pressed her face into the pillow and sobbed.

Sheriff Fritz Javor shook his head, then ran his thick fingers through his thinning brown hair. He was a tall, broad man in his late thirties and he felt sorry for the Hewitts, real sorry, as they reported their little girl missing. He had a kid, a twelve-year-old boy, and he didn't know what he would do if Bruce turned up missing. Bruce lived with his mother. That that's the way it should be with Fritz being Sheriff and on call day or night. He leaned across his desk and looked right at the Hewitts. "We'll do all we can, folks, but that's not much. We don't have the manpower that the city folk have. But we will send out the girl's description right away. You know your little girl just might turn up on your doorstep by supper." He was hungry and looking forward to eating with Kate. She never asked anything of him that he couldn't give, not like Noreen had.

Leta shook her head and gripped her purse tightly in her lap. "We told you what Miss Foley and the kids at school said. Someone took Ann. I know it!"

"Now, Miss Foley didn't see the girl get in the car

and she didn't know if the man was a friend or a stranger."

Morgan ground his teeth. Why didn't the man jump on this and do something? "Isn't there some way you can check the man out?"

Fritz sighed, trying to stay patient, but he wasn't a patient man. "Just how would we do that? Miss Foley didn't give a very good description of the man. We can send what we got through the computer and we can check on known felons, but that's not going to do much for you tonight. I told you our computer's down. We got a couple people working on it, but that doesn't mean it'll be fixed before morning." He rubbed his hand across his face and his whiskers sounded raspy. He would have to shave before going to Kate's. What a bother it was to have such a heavy growth of whiskers. Why, some guys could go two days without shaving. Then all they had to do was rub a little cream on and let the cat lick it off—whiskers and all.

Morgan moved restlessly on the straight-backed chair. "We don't know what else to do. We talked to our families and our neighbors and the babysitter." His anger rose and almost choked him as he thought about Sally. "We talked to teachers and students. We don't know what else to do. We can't just go home and sit quietly and wait."

"We won't!" cried Leta with a flip of her head.

"I hear you, folks. I do, and I'd feel the same if my kid was missing, but there's just not much I can do right now. But I will do all I can. If the girl turns up tonight, call me, okay?"

Leta jumped up, her blue eyes flashing. "Ann is her name! Ann Louise Hewitt! She's only nine years old and she's not home where she belongs!"

Morgan covered his face with shaking hands. He

couldn't take much more.

Fritz looked from one to the other, then sighed heavily. "I don't usually do this, but I'll give you a name."

Morgan jumped up and stood beside Leta across the cluttered desk from Sheriff Javor. Phones rang on the other side of the room on other cluttered desks. "What name?" Morgan asked. "Who is it?"

"It's a private detective I know. Does good work. Lives a few miles out of town going toward Freburg." He scribbled the name, address and phone number of both home and office. "Here. It's up to you. You might not feel like you need a private detective. But then again, you might."

Morgan grabbed the card and pushed it into his shirt pocket. "We'll take all the help we can get."

Fritz watched them walk out and leaned back with a tired sigh. He should have been a street cleaner, not a cop. Things like this hit too close to home and it hurt.

On the sidewalk Leta spun around to face Morgan. Cars drove up and down the street. "Show me the card. Let's go right now!"

He pulled the card from his pocket as he walked toward the car. Cold wind blew against him and he shivered. He knew he really couldn't afford a detective, but he'd find a way.

Leta jerked the card from his fingers and read, "Amber Ainslie."

"Amber?" Morgan peered at the card. "I know Amber Ainslie."

"You do?"

"Yes. Amber Ainslie. She'll help us. I know she will."

Leta frowned. Something about the way he looked sent jealousy raging inside her. "Do I know her?"

"I think so. Great girl. Real pretty red hair," said Morgan softly.

"I remember her! You went out with her a few times your senior year of high school." Her voice rose and she sounded as jealous as she felt.

He turned to Leta. "Maybe you should stay home in case Ann does show up."

Leta shook her head. "I'm going with you. Mom and Dad are at our place and we can call regularly to see if Ann is there."

"Are you sure?"

Leta nodded grimly.

Morgan squeezed her arm as he opened her car door.

Chapter 6

Amber Ainslie kicked off her black heels, tucked her black gathered skirt up against the back of her legs and sat cross-legged on the floor. The coffee table held her supper—a chef salad with large chunks of mild cheese and pieces of turkey. She touched the worn carpet. "At least it's clean," she said. She glanced around at the sparsely furnished room. Contemporary gospel music played on her tape deck. She really had gone overboard on her sound system, but she loved good sound. The rest of the room looked pretty tacky. She shrugged. It was only a stopping-off place for her until she could buy a house in the country.

She closed her eyes and said, "Heavenly Father, I'm thankful for what I have. Thank you for your great blessings to me and thank you for this wonderful salad. It is blessed to my body in Jesus' name. Amen!"

She laughed as she stabbed a piece of turkey. Wild masses of bright red hair curled down her back and cascaded over her slender shoulders to touch the strands of gold chains that Dad had given her for her twenty-seventh birthday.

She stopped chewing and sighed heavily. Dad had really messed up his life with Mom. Would they ever get back together? "I will never get divorced!"

She had prayed for God to send the right man to her. When He did she would work at making the marriage last forever.

Slowly she finished her salad. She stifled a yawn. She was tired and looked forward to making a hot fudge sundae sprinkled with nuts. Finally she could relax with the book she was trying to finish and listen to her music. She smiled. The case was closed. "Successfully, I might add," she said with a chuckle. "Now, I can rest and look for my house."

She wanted a small but elegant house in the country surrounded by trees. Maybe a log cabin. In the past five years she had saved enough for a substantial down payment and it was beginning to burn a hole in her pocket. She could also look for property and have a house built. That way she would get everything she wanted.

Just then she heard a sound from the other side of the wall where her landlady lived. "I *have* to get away from her," Amber muttered as she jumped up. "She is too nosy for me and for my kind of work."

She glanced toward the window, half expecting to see Mina Streebe peeking in. Mina had the crazy idea that private detectives lived glamorous lives twenty-four hours a day. She was determined to be included in Amber's life.

At the counter Amber scooped out French vanilla ice cream, poured hot fudge sauce over it and sprinkled it with pecan pieces. "Lookin' good!" she said as she held it high. Her day was complete when she had her hot fudge sundae. The past few days she'd been too busy and too tired to fix one.

She sank to the floor beside the tape deck and smiled. "Good music and a hot fudge sundae. What can beat that?" Lifting the first bite to her mouth, she closed her eyes to enjoy the taste of the creamy hot fudge mixed with the cold ice cream.

Someone knocked and she frowned. Maybe Mina Streebe wanted to come in and watch her eat her sundae. She laughed and took another bite.

Someone knocked again. Reluctantly she jumped up, set the sundae on the counter and walked to the door. She would make a sundae for Mina too.

She flung open the door, ready to ask Mina if she wanted ice cream. The words died in her throat as she looked at the worried man and woman standing there.

"Hello, Amber," said the man.

She gasped. "Morgan! Morgan Hewitt! What in the world brings you here?" She turned to the woman. "Leta? Leta Stanley? Come in! It's wonderful to see you both! Leta, I worked for your dad one summer stocking shelves. How is he?"

"We came on business," said Leta. "Sheriff Javor said you'd help us." She hadn't expected Amber to remember her. But then Amber always had been a very outgoing, caring person. "Something terrible has happened."

Amber closed the door and studied Morgan and Leta. They looked old for their years, very tired and very frightened. "Tell me about it."

Morgan stabbed his fingers through his dark hair. "We have a little girl. Ann. She's missing."

"Oh, I'm so sorry!" Amber motioned for them to sit on the love seat and she pulled up a straight chair. "You don't mind if I record this, do you?"

"No," said Morgan, and Leta shook her head.

Amber clicked off her music, slipped in an empty cassette and pushed Record. "With this I don't miss any important details that you might tell me. Now, start at the beginning and tell me all about it."

Quickly Morgan and Leta told the story. Occasionally Amber asked a question.

When they finished, Amber asked, "What does she look like and what was she wearing this morning when she left the house?"

"She's nine, small for her age, with blond hair to her shoulders, wide blue eyes." Leta's voice broke.

"She's such a tiny little thing," said Morgan. "She loves people but sometimes she's shy."

"She loves bananas," whispered Leta. In a trembling voice she described her jacket, jeans and blouse. "She wore her old sneakers today because she said kids would make fun of her if she had on new ones."

Amber glanced at the tape deck to make sure it was still recording. It was. She had listened carefully to every detail. She knew she was good at her job but she was surprised that Fritz Javor had given the Hewitts her name, and especially her private address. It wasn't like him at all. She would ask him later what he had in mind.

Several minutes later Amber said, "I will do everything I can to find Ann. You two let me know if you hear from anyone or if Ann comes home. That does happen, you know. Do you have my office number and address?"

"The sheriff gave it to us," said Morgan, patting the card in his pocket. He felt better knowing Amber was on the case. She always was one to get a job done.

"How soon will you find Ann?" asked Leta.

"I don't know, Leta, but I do know I'll do all I can to find her."

Tears sparkled in Leta's eyes. "Thank you."

Morgan stood up. "We want to get home in case Ann is there."

"Oh, I hope she is!" Leta glanced toward the phone. "Could I call to see?"

Amber nodded and Leta dialed the number and waited for someone to answer. She heard her dad's voice and couldn't speak for a moment. "Is Ann there, Daddy?"

"No." Burl sounded close to tears.

"We'll be home soon." Leta hung up and turned to Morgan, her face more haggard than before. "She's not there."

He slipped his arm around her and pulled her close to his side. "Let's go home."

"I'll be praying," said Amber.

"Thanks," said Morgan. He remembered that Amber had always been strong in faith.

Amber walked them to the door. Just as she reached to open it, someone knocked.

Leta jerked back with a strangled scream.

Morgan pulled her back to his side. "Easy, honey," he whispered.

She nodded. "I want my baby," she said with a sob.

Amber opened the door. Mina Streebe stood there with a grin on her round face. Mina was short and plump with wild gray hair. She wore a bright flowered blouse with red slacks. "Hello, Mina," said Amber with a sigh. "What can I do for you?"

"I came to see who was here." Mina tried to look past Amber, but Amber blocked the door.

"They're friends of mine and they're just leaving," said Amber.

Mina's face fell. "Oh, I thought I was going to get in on an exciting caper. Too bad."

"Too bad," said Amber. She said goodbye to Morgan and Leta and watched them walk to their car. The bright yard light lit the way for them. Stars twinkled in the sky. A nippy breeze made Amber shiver.

"Could I come in for a while?" asked Mina with a shiver.

"I do have work to do. I don't want to be rude, but I am too busy for a chat right now. Another time, okay?"

Mina's face fell. "I sure thought I was going to get in on something big. I sure did." She walked back to her door, muttering under her breath.

Chuckling, Amber closed the door. "Poor Mina. She needs to find something interesting to do with her life now that her husband is dead and she's retired."

Amber picked up her sundae, ate the fudge and nuts and washed the melted ice cream down the drain. She washed and dried the few dishes, slipped into jeans, a warm pink sweater and sneakers. After wearing heels all day the sneakers felt good on her feet. She sat on the floor and replayed the tape of the Hewitts. Clicking it off, she sat with her knees pulled to her chin, her arms around her legs.

"Heavenly Father, you know all things and you've created me with great reasoning powers. Help me with this case as you've helped me with my others. Show me how and where to find Ann Hewitt. Keep her safe. Comfort Morgan and Leta. Thanks for your help. Thank you for hearing and answering. I love you and I always want to glorify you. In Jesus' name, Amen."

She jumped up with a smile, her earlier weariness completely gone. She would go to her office and see what she could find on the computer.

Grabbing her leather jacket out of the closet Amber slipped it on as she walked out the door. She heard the lock click and smiled. She had the locks changed to keep Mina out of her place. Amber glanced at Mina's window. Wouldn't Mina be surprised when her key wouldn't work in the lock?

Amber slipped into her silver-blue Buick, drove

out of the narrow driveway to the highway and turned toward Freburg. Where was Ann tonight?

Several minutes later Amber ran toward the office complex where several offices were lit up. Others were also working late tonight. As she unlocked the office and stepped inside she sighed, "So much for a quiet night of reading." Her evening would be spent at the computer checking on known child molesters. Maybe she could match a description with the one the Hewitts had given her.

Several blocks away Ann lay on her side sleeping with her legs pulled up tightly against her body and the covers over her. Tears had dried on her face, but the pillow was still damp.

Sam stood at the sink with his hands in the hot, sudsy water. He was washing the piles of dishes. When he left for work in the morning Ann wouldn't need to face a dirty room. Not that she would object to the mess. She was a good little girl to have around. Once she had stopped crying, he had fun talking to her, telling her all about himself and his job and his future plans. He hadn't told her about the three terrible years in prison or about his mother and two sisters.

He hummed softly as he scoured a plate. He glanced over at the TV just in time to watch a chase scene. Finally he turned back to the dishes. Later he would relax on the couch and watch TV as late as he wanted. Tonight, and every night that Ann was visiting him, he'd sleep on the couch. He would not touch Ann and he would not hurt her. He had learned his lesson.

Morgan stared out of the living room window as he listened to Leta and her parents talking in the kitchen. He knew they wanted to say goodnight to Leta alone. There was still no word of Ann. She wouldn't be home to sleep in her own bed tonight. Where was she sleeping? Or was she dead? Tears stung Morgan's eyes and he wiped them away.

He walked to the doorway of Ann's room and clicked on the light. Stuffed bears ranging from thumb size to almost his size decorated the blue and white room. A pair of little black dress shoes peeked out from under the dresser. A pink rabbit lay on the chair at her desk. "Oh, Ann," he whispered.

Leta touched his arm and he jumped. "Want a cup of tea?"

"She should be sleeping right here, Leta."

"I know."

He leaned against the door frame with his head down. "Where is she tonight? Is she safe?"

"Amber said she would help us find her."

He clicked off the bedroom light and walked away from it. "It hurts too much to see that empty bed."

She rubbed his arm. "Let's have a cup of tea, Morgan."

Finally he nodded. Just then the phone rang and they both jumped and raced to the kitchen to grab it. Morgan's hand closed over the receiver first. He barked into the phone.

"Any word on Ann, Morgan?" Dolly asked.

Morgan sagged against the wall. "No, Mom. No word."

Leta sank against the counter, her head down.

"But we hired Amber Ainslie. Remember her, Mom? She's a private detective now and she said she will help us find Ann."

"I'm glad, Morgan. You and Leta keep trusting God to answer. Get some rest tonight so you'll be fresh for tomorrow. I love you and so does your dad."

He talked a few more minutes while Leta set the teakettle on to boil.

Several minutes later they sat at the table sipping tea. Silence pressed against Morgan. He thought of the soothing music at Amber's and walked to the living room and clicked in the new Phil Driscoll tape.

Morgan sank to the couch and Leta hesitated, then sat beside him. Without talking they listened to the music. He turned his head and found her studying him. Their eyes locked and he couldn't turn away, nor did he want to. Her heart skipped a beat.

"I don't want to be alone tonight," he said softly.

"Neither do I," she whispered.

Morgan slipped an arm around her and she leaned her head against his shoulder. He closed his eyes and drew comfort from her and from the music. Why had he pulled away from God? Morgan leaned his head against Leta's sweet smelling hair. He didn't realize how cold he'd become toward God until he and Leta had separated. Then it had been too hard to pray. He had allowed room in his life for Satan to destroy his marriage and his daughter. Just how long would he put up with that?

A dam burst inside and Morgan silently cried out for God to forgive him and help him. As he prayed, a peace he hadn't felt in a long time settled over him.

The doorbell chimed. He jumped up with Leta close beside him.

"Could it be Ann?" asked Leta.

He flung wide the door.

Leta saw Ben and Denise Ogden standing there, their eyes full of love and concern. Leta sagged against the wall.

"We came to tell you that we're thinking of you," said Ben.

"Come in, pastor," said Morgan.

Denise stepped inside and gathered Leta close in her arms. "We've been praying," whispered Denise.

Leta's eyes overflowed as she pulled away. "Thank you."

"The prayer chain is praying around the clock," said Ben.

"Thank you and thank them," said Morgan. "Can you come in and sit a while?"

"We don't want to intrude," said Ben. "We just wanted you to know you have our support. Call us night or day if you need anything."

"We mean it," said Denise as she patted Leta's arm.

Leta thought of the times she had wanted to confide in Denise. Maybe one of these days she could do so.

Denise smiled from Morgan to Leta. "Just remember that God is a help in time of trouble. He never leaves you nor forsakes you. With God you are more than conquerors."

"Find the promises in the Scriptures and cling to them," said Ben.

"We will," said Morgan, and he meant it.

They talked a while longer, prayed in a circle, and Leta held the door while Ben and Denise walked out. Cool wind blew in. Sounds of traffic blended together with the sound of Phil Driscoll singing on the tape player. Leta brushed tears from her eyes as she slowly closed the door.

Morgan studied her face. "Leta?"

Her stomach fluttered. She couldn't trust her voice, so she lifted her brow questioningly.

"Do you want me to stay?"

Could she survive if she said yes and he said he'd rather go back to his place? "Do you want to stay?"

He did, but what if she really didn't want him? "I don't want to be alone."

"Neither do I."

"Then I'll stay." Slowly he slipped his arms around her. She stiffened then leaned against him. He held her closer until he felt her heartbeat against his. She clung to him and breathed in his special scent. Oh, it was good to be in his arms again!

Chapter 7

Amber dropped the print-out on her desk and sighed loud and long. She tapped the stack. "Known child molesters. What of the unknowns?" She leaned back against her chair. What of all the creeps who walked the streets and malls looking for children to carry away to unknown places, never to be heard from again?

She glanced at her gold watch, then leaned back and closed her eyes. "One A.M. and still awake," she muttered. She had contacted all the hospitals within a three-hundred mile radius, but none of them had an unknown of Ann's description. She had sent the description to Missing Children along with her number and the Hewitts'.

Soft music filled the room from the tape deck beside her four-drawer files. Plants hung on a plant tree near the door to her secretary's office. The room smelled of paper and apple 'n spice potpourri.

Amber reached for the phone. "Fritz, are you home yet?" She had tried every hour on the hour to reach him. If she didn't get him this time, she would drive home, take a warm shower and try again. On the third ring he picked it up.

"Javor here." He stifled a yawn, then tugged his shirttail from his pants.

"Fritz, I hope I'm not bothering you." She laughed.

"Then again, I hope I am."

"You always bother me, Amber."

"This is important."

"It's kind of late, isn't it?" He unbuttoned his shirt, sank to the edge of the couch, and stretched out his long legs. He was tired and wanted to go to bed, but he had expected to hear from her before the night was over. He should have called her from Kate's. "What can I do for you, Amber?"

"As if you didn't know." She leaned forward, her arm on her desk, her fingers drumming the print-out. "What's the word on the Hewitts?"

"It might not be anything, but then again . . ."

"What, Fritz?" She gripped the receiver tightly. An ambulance siren wailed as it drove past.

"You at the office?"

"Yes."

"You got Sam Walcott on your print-out?"

She sorted through. "Yes." Butterflies fluttered in her stomach. "He's been in for rape. A ten-year-old girl." Amber closed her eyes and forced back the pricks of fear.

"It might not mean anything, but I saw the guy in town a few weeks ago. He's short, he's slight, but he had no beard. But he could've grown one, or glued one on." Fritz jerked his legs up and narrowed his eyes into twin blue slits. "Go easy with this one, Amber. He's sick. I mean SICK! He should have been put away for good, but he puts on a good act, knows the right words to say to the psychiatrist, and the system stinks. He's walking the streets as free as you and me."

"I get a bad feeling just thinking about him."

"Tell me about it."

"That's why you sent the Hewitts to me?"

"That's why." He chuckled softly. "Besides, I

thought you might be tired of looking for your perfect dream house by now and would want a job."

"Sure, sure."

"And our computer was down and we don't have the manpower."

Amber tapped her pencil on the desk. "I have not had time to look for my dream house, Fritz."

"Too bad."

"Do you know of anything available?"

"Mine."

"Not true, Fritz. Your place is a pig sty."

"Amber, I'm crushed." He looked around at the mess.

"Besides, you don't want to marry me, and I have marriage in mind."

"Ha, ha."

"Don't panic. I know the thought of marriage terrifies you. And you, a big grown man."

"One bad marriage is enough for me, thanks."

She was silent a long time. "Fritz?"

"Yah?"

"Would this guy, this Sam Walcott just rape her and let her go?"

"You tell me."

Amber read the file. "The last time he kept the girl at his place for almost a week. She was nearly dead when they found her."

"And to think he's walking the streets again."

"Can't you *do* anything?"

He cleared his throat and rammed his fingers through his thinning hair. "I drove over to his address in Freburg which is out of my jurisdiction and knocked on his door, just to say hello, you know."

"And?" Her shoulder muscles knotted with tension.

"And he wasn't there. He moved and left no forwarding address. His parole officer doesn't have a new address for him."

"Oh, Fritz!"

"I know."

"What if I spend all my time tracking down Sam Walcott and it turns out he's not our man? All that time would be wasted and Ann could be dead or worse."

"I know."

Amber drew a thick checkmark beside Sam Walcott's name. "I have his psychiatrist's number. I'll give him a call in the morning. Bright and early."

"Bright and early comes earlier for some people. You'd better get home and hit the sack."

"I know."

"Good night, Amber."

"Fritz, did you know that I once dated Morgan Hewitt?"

His dark brows shot up. "You don't say!"

"His senior year of high school."

"He doesn't seem your type."

She laughed. "As if you knew my type. He seemed so tense, so worn out."

"Getting your kid taken can do that to you."

"I know." Amber closed her eyes. "I want to find his little girl for him."

"For old time's sake?"

"I want to put a smile back on his face and a light in his eyes."

"His wife needs a smile on her face, too. You ever think about that?"

"Yes. And about Ann." Tears blurred Amber's vision. "You know something, Fritz?"

"What?"

"I'm tired, real tired and if I don't get to bed I'll be crying all over this telephone."

"Me, too, honey. Let me know if I can help."

"And you let *me* know if you learn anything, like where Sam Walcott lives now."

"Will do, Amber. We'll get on it first thing."

"With all of us working together, we'll find her before long." She waited for his response but none came. "Right, Fritz?"

"Right, Red." He shook his head and wearily rubbed a large hand over his wide forehead. "Right. Go home and go to bed. It's been a long day."

"Yah."

"Sleep tight, Red."

"You too, Fritz." Slowly she hung up and then sat there with her head bowed. It had been a long day and it was almost a half-hour drive to her place. Too bad Dr. Nolen Grant had an unlisted phone number. Some things had to wait for morning and this was one of them.

Cold sweat covered Leta's body and she jerked up in bed, gripping the top sheet with both hands. She trembled. Street lights cast a soft glow over the room. Morgan reached for her in his sleep. She touched his bare shoulder then shook him. "Morgan, wake up!"

He shot bolt upright. He saw the terror on Leta's face. "What's wrong, honey?"

"I dreamed I saw Ann!"

"Oh, Leta." He gathered her close but she struggled free.

"Morgan, it was terrible. Just awful."

"Do you want to talk about it?" He saw her shiver and he wrapped her robe around her shoulders.

"I saw her. Ann. I saw her in my dream." Leta plucked at the sheet. "She was caught . . . caught in a tear. Caught in a giant teardrop! Oh, Morgan, she was trying to break out but she couldn't. She looked frantic. I tried to help her and I couldn't!"

He saw the picture she painted with words and he shivered too. "It was only a dream, Leta."

"But it seemed so real."

"We know she's been very unhappy about our separation. You probably felt that and knew that wherever she is tonight she's frightened, so in your dream the two were put together."

She nodded. "I want her back! I want to help her!"

"Praying will help."

"I know," she whispered.

Morgan held her close and prayed.

Wanda Stanley shivered as she paced the living room. She glanced down at her bare feet and suddenly realized she hadn't slipped on her robe or her slippers. In a daze she picked up the afghan that Morgan's mother had knitted for her and slipped it around her, holding it together with her arms clasped across her breast.

How could Burl sleep knowing that little Ann was still missing? Didn't he care any more about Ann than he had about his own children?

Wanda gasped and sank weakly to an overstuffed chair. How could she think such a terrible thing? Of course Burl loved the children.

A dog barked outdoors. The house creaked. Lately she was often awake to hear the night sounds. Burl always slept on even when she needed him to wake up and hold her close.

"So, here you are!" exclaimed Burl.

She looked up and stared at Burl as he stood in the doorway with only his dress pants on, his belt hanging. "I couldn't sleep."

He frowned and looked away. "You look like an old woman with that thing wrapped around you."

Anger rushed through her. "I am not a teenager anymore, Burl. I have every right to look old!"

"What's gotten into you, woman?" He stood at the wide front window and looked out at the glow of the streetlight on the lawn. Headlights stabbed the darkness and a car drove past, leaving behind a greater darkness. Finally, he turned around. "What's wrong with you, Wanda?"

"If you don't know, I'm certainly not going to tell you." She stood up stiffly. "Why don't you just go back to bed and sleep again? Leave me in peace!" His long, thin body irritated her. She wished he had done something to develop a few muscles.

"I got as much right in my own living room as you do. More, in fact. It was my money that got us this."

She lifted her chin and her dark eyes flashed. "I hate you, Burl. Do you know that? I hate you just as much as you hate me. And you never knew it until now."

The words struck him in the gut and he sat down heavily. "You're talking nonsense, Wanda."

"Am I? Don't you think that I know why you keep me around? You're used to me. I cook your meals and keep a clean house and warm your bed."

He gripped the arms of his chair. She was right but he'd never put it into words before. "We're too old for divorce, Wanda. Sit down and talk this out before you do something crazy."

Her legs trembled and she dropped back to her chair. She wanted him to deny her angry words, not admit to them. "Divorce is quick in your thoughts, isn't it? And quick on your tongue when you talk to Leta and Morgan."

"Morgan's no good for her. He has no money!"

"He makes more money than you do."

Burl's face turned brick red. He rubbed at his bare chest and arms. "I am an important person in this town."

"Who cares?"

He stared at her in surprise. "What's come over you, Wanda?"

She clutched the afghan tighter. "I am tired of my miserable life. I have no purpose, no reason for living. And if something terrible happens to little Ann, I won't want to live another day."

"Don't talk such nonsense!"

"Sometimes I think Leta was right. Having a close personal relationship with God is the answer for everyone."

"Leta wouldn't say that today."

"Of course not! You encouraged her to give up her faith. She always wanted to please you. Do you know why, Burl? Because she knew you didn't care that much!" Wanda snapped her fingers and the sound was loud in the room.

"I don't have to sit here and take this." But he couldn't move. Why hadn't he stayed in bed? He didn't need her beside him. Although the few times she had been away from home, he couldn't sleep without her close to his side.

"Run on back to bed and pull the covers over your head, Burl. Shut out the real world. Or better yet, run to the store and get involved so you don't have to face your family and their problems. Or face me."

He curled his toes into the carpet. He hadn't realized that she understood him so well. At times he thought she was slow, even dull-witted. How wrong he was! A strange respect for her rose inside him and he looked at her as if he had never seen her before.

"You didn't care when our Ann died."

He frowned. "What are you talking about?"

She sniffed. "Our baby. Our baby who died. I named her Ann and you didn't know or care."

"That was a long time ago."

"Nineteen years."

He couldn't think of anything to say. It hadn't bothered him for long when the baby died. He thought Wanda had gotten over it easily too. After all, she had three other children.

"I'm surprised that you care that Ann Louise is missing."

"Wanda!"

"You don't care about Leta."

"I do care!"

Wanda leaned forward. "Then talk her into going back with Morgan. I want Leta and Morgan to love each other madly, passionately. I want Ann to grow up in a happy home. If she comes home."

"I don't know what's gotten into you." Burl stood up. "I'm going back to bed. Do what you want." Suddenly he was conscious of his stick-thin body, his large nose and shaggy mustache. His back stiff, he walked out of the room.

Wanda flung the afghan from her and paced in agitation. She stopped at the window. "Be safe, Ann," she whispered. "And Leta, make something wonderful of your marriage."

Dolly pulled the cover over her cold shoulder, then opened her eyes to find John kneeling beside the bed, praying in whispers. She slipped out of bed. Her silky gown fell in graceful folds to her bare feet. She knelt beside John. He turned his head and smiled.

"Help me, John. I'm suddenly very frightened for Ann."

"So was I. That's why I'm praying." He slipped his warm arm around her and kissed her. "God is for us, who can be against us? Greater is He within

us, than he that's in the world. We are more than
conquerors through Jesus Christ, our Lord. And this
is the confidence that we have in Him, that if we ask
anything according to His will, He hears us. And if
we know that He hears us, whatever we ask, we
know that we have the petitions that we desired of
Him. God is not a man that He should lie; neither
the son of man that He should repent. Has He said,
and shall He not do it? Or has He spoken and shall
He not make it good?"

Dolly smiled. "I needed that."

"So did I."

She pushed her face against the covers and prayed
for Ann.

Sally Perrin sat on the couch with her eyes glued
to the TV. The late night movie played, but all she
could see was Ann's face. She turned up the volume,
and for a minute she watched the screen.

"Why did you let her walk to school alone, Sally?"
Leta Hewitt's question rang inside Sally's head. She
covered her ears and closed her eyes. Ann's picture
was impressed on the inside of her eyelids.

Sally jumped up and looked around wildly. Suddenly she remembered Mom's sleeping tablets.

Sally clicked off the television and ran to Mom's
bedroom. Frantically she jerked open the nightstand
drawer. She rummaged through the contents and
finally found the plastic container.

"Good!" She held it to her heart and breathed
deeply.

She ran to the bathroom, filled a glass with water,
and swallowed a tablet, then another. "Now, I'll
sleep."

Walking to her bedroom, Sally slipped between
the covers and closed her eyes.

Chapter 8

Amber slapped at the alarm clock, finally opened her eyes, found the button and clicked it off. Abruptly the wicked buzzing stopped. She flopped back in place and stared toward the window where sunlight peeked through. "Seven already. How can I get up?"

Wearily she crept from bed, walked in a daze to the bathroom, then to the sound system where she clicked on her exercise tape. Music blasted the room and she jumped to turn it down. "I must really be sleepy. I didn't even know I turned the volume button."

She lifted her hands high and stretched, then touched her toes. After a couple minutes of forced routine, her body woke up. She jumped and twisted and danced the routine that she followed each morning.

Later she stood under the warm shower. Her stomach growled. She would grab a banana instead of fixing eggs and an English muffin with tea.

She pulled a bright green cotton dress from her closet and slipped it over her head. It hugged her curves as she added a wide belt. She blew her hair dry, put on makeup with quick, expert strokes, then picked up her Bible to read. Just as she finished reading, someone knocked.

With a frown she opened the door. Mina Streebe breezed in with a covered tray in her hands.

"I saw you get in at two this morning. I knew you wouldn't have time to fix a healthy breakfast, so I made you some." Mina set the tray on the table and whisked off the cloth.

Amber stared at the wedges of cantaloupe, English muffins with an egg and a cup of tea. "Why thank you, Mina. Would you like to join me?"

"Sure!" Mina tugged her huge red sweater down over her red slacks. She dropped into the chair across from Amber. "Tell me all about your new case."

Amber stabbed a piece of cantaloupe. "You know I can't tell you about it."

Mina tapped her toe and frowned. "I can help you, you know. All my life I wanted to be a detective. I studied how to solve crime. I read all the detective books I could find in the library. I've watched every detective series on TV. I know how to do deductive reasoning. I can sort through clues and find the important, meaningful ones."

Amber ate quickly, then stood up. "You can stay and watch me brush my teeth if you want, but then I must go."

Mina's round shoulders slumped. "All right, all right. I'll go but you don't know what you're missing by not accepting my help."

"I'm sure I don't." Amber smiled and Mina slowly walked out with her head down.

Several minutes later Amber turned her car toward Bradsville. She wanted to talk to the Hewitts before driving to Freburg to talk with Dr. Grant. Maybe he would shed light on Sam Walcott's whereabouts and actions.

After the Hewitts learned Amber's news, Leta asked, "Could I get you a cup of coffee, Amber?"

"No, thanks, Leta. I'd like to look at Ann's room."

"Why?" asked Morgan as they led Amber to the room.

"I want to get a feel of Ann. There might be something that will help me."

In Ann's room Amber looked at the stuffed bears. "What a collection!"

"She's been collecting bears since she was five," said Morgan.

"My mother started her on it," said Leta, touching the panda on the bed. "This was her first bear."

Amber looked in the closet and found that Ann preferred jeans over dresses.

Leta stood near the bed and watched Amber look around. Leta caught a glimpse of herself in the mirror and frowned. She looked drab and dull next to Amber's brilliance. Leta touched the wide barrettes that held back her brown hair. She tugged her fuzzy pink sweater over her dark blue slacks. She was not able to cover the dark smudges under her eyes with makeup. She peeked at Morgan as he studied Ann's bulletin board. Did he notice how gorgeous Amber was and how plain Leta was? She bit back a low groan.

Morgan walked listlessly around the room. After Leta's nightmare he had stayed awake staring at the ceiling and listening to Leta breathe. Finally he slipped from the bed and sat in the living room listening to music. About five he dropped off the sleep, only to waken at seven. He had called Queens to let them know he couldn't make it to work.

Pushing his hands into his pockets, he hunched his broad shoulders. He felt rumpled and old. He needed a shave and a change of clothes.

"Do you have a recent photo of Ann I can take?" asked Amber.

Leta pulled one out of an album on the desk. "This is the latest one we have."

Amber gripped the photo and looked down at the smiling girl with pretty blond shoulder-length hair. Her wide blue eyes were the same color as the background. She wore a pink blouse with puffy sleeves.

Just how much longer would Ann look this pretty? If someone had picked her up, how long would she stay alive? Amber's heart jerked.

"That's the same blouse that she wore yesterday," said Leta in a strangled voice.

"Find her for us, Amber," whispered Morgan.

Amber nodded. She hadn't told them about Sam Walcott. "I'll keep in touch. God is with us. Remember that."

Several minutes later she stopped at the school to talk to Marilyn Foley.

At the Hewitts, Morgan pulled his car keys out of his pocket and jangled them. The noise startled him and he caught them in his hand and held them tightly.

"Where are you going?" asked Leta in alarm.

"To get a change of clothes. I'll be right back."

"Don't leave me alone! Please!" She clung to his arm.

He nodded. "We'll get Mabel from next door to come and stay by the phone."

"Thank you!" How had she forgotten that he was so kind and thoughtful? His kindness had attracted her attention in the first place.

He rubbed his raspy jaw. "I need a shave." What would she say if he told her that he wanted to pack up everything and move back home?

Later Leta watched Morgan pack a few things in his bag. She opened her mouth to ask if he'd pack everything and come back home for good, but she couldn't force the words out. He might reject her and right now she couldn't handle that.

While he shaved she stood in the doorway and watched just as she had hundreds of times.

"We'll stop at the newspaper office and drop off the picture of Ann," said Leta, touching her purse where she'd slipped the photo. "I called Martin and he said he would run it on the first page."

"I'll get some posters printed and pass them around in all the stores." Morgan patted his face dry. "What time are we scheduled at the TV station in Grand Rapids?"

"Eleven." She shuddered.

He pulled her close and held her. She smelled his aftershave and felt the smooth skin of his face. Oh, how she'd missed him! "Leta, are you sure you can handle the interview?"

"I can't, but I must. I'll do anything to get Ann back."

"Me too." He ran a finger lightly down her cheek. He'd made a mistake by walking out on her. "It seems we're all caught in a tear."

She nodded. "Just like Ann."

Amber parked so she could watch Dr. Grant's special parking space. She leaned back with a sigh. Her talks with Marilyn Foley and with Sally Perrin hadn't been much help. But Dr. Grant should be full of helpful information. In just a few hours maybe this would all be wrapped up with Ann back home and Sam Walcott behind bars again.

"Amber, Amber, you're not doing an hour-long TV series here, you know." Amber chuckled. She rolled down the car window and let in the warm spring air. Cars whizzed past on the busy street beside the medical building. What if this was a waste of time? Ann Hewitt might be hiding in a neighbor's garage to try to get her parents back together. Amber sighed heavily. Sam Walcott was a lead that she had to follow even if he had nothing to do with Ann.

Amber tapped her steering wheel impatiently. "Where are you, Dr. Grant?"

Just then a black Cadillac drove into Dr. Grant's space. A tall, good looking man with a neatly trimmed black beard and mustache stepped out. Amber slipped from her car and walked toward him, her heels tapping on the pavement.

"Dr. Grant," she called.

He turned with a frown, then smiled when he saw her. "Yes? What can I do for you?"

"I'm Amber Ainslie, Doctor, and I need a few minutes of your time. To talk about Sam Walcott."

Nolen Grant's face closed and he dusted off his immaculate sleeve. "Do you have an appointment to see me?"

"No. I'm a detective and I must find Sam Walcott."

"I can't help you." He turned away but she caught his arm. He looked down at her slender hand and shell-pink nails, then into her beautiful face. "I can't help you."

"There's a nine-year-old girl missing. Sam Walcott was seen in her area. I must talk to him. He moved and the parole officer doesn't have his new address."

Dr. Grant shook his head. "You have the wrong man. Sam's been coming to me for a while now and he's doing just fine. He wouldn't abduct a girl again. I know. Take my word for it."

"You're sure?"

He nodded.

"Enough to stake a little girl's life on it?"

He frowned. "I'll give you his address, but he's

not your man. He's handling his frustrations. No. He's not your man."

Amber walked to his office and thankfully took the address he gave her. She read it quickly, then frowned. "This is his old address, Dr. Grant."

Nolen Grant snatched the paper from Amber, wadded it and flung it into the wicker wastebasket. "It seems that I can't help you at all. I have a patient waiting for me. You may leave by my private door."

She lifted her chin and her eyes flashed. "When is Sam Walcott's next appointment?"

Nolen Grant hesitated, then glanced at his calendar. "Friday at ten."

"If you hear from him before then, call me." She pulled her card from her purse and held it out to him.

He took it and dropped in on his desk.

She strode from the room and into the hallway. It smelled of medicine and cleaning supplies. Maybe she would get Fritz to give the good doctor a call.

She found a pay phone in the lobby of the medical building and dialed Fritz at his office.

Fritz held a cup of coffee in one hand and a danish in the other. The phone rang and he scowled at it. It rang again. Finally he answered.

"I want you to rake Dr. Nolen Grant over the coals, Fritz. He won't give me anything except to say that Sam Walcott couldn't be guilty of taking the girl."

"He could be right, Red."

"What? How can you say that after giving me his name?"

"I just got a call. Not more than an hour ago. I tried to reach you." He cleared his throat and she felt the tension over the wire. "Amber, a frightened woman from Sidney called to report that a man is holding a child against her will at his place. The girl is blond and young. It could be Ann Hewitt."

Amber closed her eyes and took a deep breath. Cigar smoke from a man walking past almost choked her. "Is she still alive?"

"We're checking it out, Red. But I thought you'd want to know." He gave her the address and she scribbled it on a small pad from her purse.

"Thanks, Fritz."

"Be careful, Red. Tell Captain Rogers that I gave you permission to be there."

"Will do." She slammed down the receiver and ran to her car, her heart racing. Maybe she could call the Hewitts before their eleven o'clock appearance on TV and tell them she had Ann safely with her. She shivered. "Please, God, protect little Ann Hewitt."

An hour later Amber stood beside Captain Rogers as paramedics carried the girl from the white frame house. Amber forced back the bitter taste that filled her mouth. The girl's face was bruised and blood oozed from a cut on her cheek.

Two officers hauled a heavy-set man from the house and pushed him into the back seat of a squad car. People from the neighborhood pushed in close and Captain Rogers shouted for them to move back. Amber walked to the ambulance. She saw the girl move her head and heard her moan.

"Wait," said Amber to the men. They shot a look at Captain Rogers and he nodded. Amber leaned close to the girl as her eyes fluttered open. "Hi. You're safe now. Soon you'll be with your family."

"I want Momma," whispered the girl through cracked lips.

"We'll get her. What's your name?"

The girl moved and moaned again.

"Tell me your name," whispered Amber.

"Jenny. Jenny Adams."

Amber sucked in her breath. "Jenny, Captain Rogers will get your mother right away. Can you tell us your address?"

Slowly Jenny recited her address.

Amber patted Jenny's hand. Where was Ann Hewitt and what condition was she in right now?

Sally Perrin walked wearily to the couch and sat down, her head in her hands. How could that private detective think that she had anything to do with Ann's disappearance? Why would she want anything bad to happen to Ann?

Sally jumped up and clicked on the TV to cover the terrible silence. A picture of Ann flashed on the screen. Sally gasped, her hand to her heart as she listened to Leta and Morgan plead for anyone to please call if they knew where Ann was.

Abruptly Sally clicked off the TV. The silence pressed against her. She locked her hands behind her back and paced the room. She stopped at the window and looked out to see if Mom was back from Detroit. "She won't come home until this afternoon."

Tears burned Sally's eyes and slipped down her ashen cheeks. Slowly she walked to Mom's bedroom and opened the nightstand drawer. The bottle of sleeping tablets rested against a brush. She picked it up and poured out the tablets, picked out one and put the rest back. The two tablets last night had put her out until Amber Ainslie had rung the doorbell almost off the side of the house this morning. One sleeping tablet now should put her out until Mom got home.

She stared at herself in the dresser mirror. "Why

didn't I walk Ann to school yesterday? Why?" She tipped her head back and screamed at the top of her lungs. Her throat ached.

Sally ran to the bathroom for a glass of water. She swallowed the tablet in one gulp.

Was Ann dead?

Sally pressed her sweaty hands to her face and trembled so hard she almost fell. Slowly she walked to her room and dropped onto the unmade bed.

She whimpered against her pillow until finally she fell asleep.

Wanda Stanley sank to the carpet in front of her TV as the picture of Ann flashed off. Tears poured down Wanda's sunken cheeks and dripped onto her legs. Was Ann alive? Or was she dead?

Weakly Wanda walked to the phone. Dare she call Burl at work so he'd come home? She shook her head. He'd never come home just to comfort her.

"What am I going to do?" She touched the afghan that Morgan's mother had made for her and hope leaped inside her. "I'll call Dolly!"

Her hands shook as she flipped through the phone book to John Hewitt. She dialed and at the sound of Dolly's voice Wanda burst into tears.

"Dolly, it's Wanda. Wanda Stanley. I need you."

Dolly sagged against the counter. She had thought for sure it was Morgan with news of Ann. "Wanda, I could come in right now if you want."

"Yes. Do. Please do."

"Just hang on, Wanda, and remember that God is our strength. I believe with all my heart that He's watching over our little Ann."

Wanda closed her eyes. "I needed to hear that."

"Me too, Wanda. See you in a few minutes."

"Dolly, thank you!"

Leta clung to Morgan's hand as they walked from the TV station to the car. "Don't you think someone will call soon with news of Ann?"

He nodded. "We'll get right home to answer the calls. We don't want poor Mabel to answer all of them." They had been told to expect several calls, some of them crank calls. But one of them could be the real thing. All of this publicity was worthwhile if it would help bring Ann back.

As they drove through Freburg Leta said, "Are you hungry?"

"A little. You?"

She nodded. She wasn't really, but she knew they had to eat something. "We could stop at the Burger King up ahead."

Morgan nodded.

A few minutes later they stood at the counter and ordered two Whoppers and fries.

Sam Walcott turned away from the deep-fryer and looked toward the counter. A tired-looking man and women stood there ordering. Sam sighed and dabbed sweat off his forehead. The lunch rush was over and he could relax a little. He smiled and his pulse leaped. Soon it would be time to go home to Ann. She might smile for him. He'd take her fries and a shake, and maybe even a Whopper.

He hummed to himself as he filled a container with fries.

Chapter 9

Leta held the receiver to her ear and listened in horror.

"If you were any kind of mother at all, you'd a been home to walk your little girl to school. God is punishing you for working." The woman's voice rose and Leta winced, then slapped down the receiver and turned to Morgan with a whimper.

"What is it?" he asked in alarm.

She clung to him, unable to speak. She knew there would be calls like this, but she wasn't prepared for it. Finally she lifted her face to Morgan and told him what the woman had said. "I should have been home with Ann. I had no business being at work when she needed me. It's my fault that she's gone!"

"No! No, it is not!" He rubbed his hands down her arms. "Don't do this to yourself. You're a wonderful mother to Ann. It's not your fault that she was taken." But maybe it was. Or maybe it was his fault for leaving home and moving into an apartment. "I wish now we wouldn't have given out our home number. They warned us not to, but I wouldn't listen."

She rubbed her hand across her nose. "None of the calls helped. None of them!"

"Maybe someone at the TV station or the police have heard something important. I should find out."

"They said they would call if anything came in."

He tugged at his collar. "I know, but maybe they couldn't get through. Our phone has been busy." He dialed the TV station's number.

She stood beside him, her icy hands locked around his arm, her eyes wide. She could tell by his response and the look on his face that nothing had come in about Ann. Tears burned her eyes and she sank to a chair. The late afternoon sun shone through the window onto the plants hanging there. The doorbell rang and she jumped up and ran to answer it.

She stared in shock at the tall, blond woman standing in the doorway. Leta wanted to slam the door in the woman's face, but she stepped back and said, "Come in, Karen."

"I came to tell you how sorry I am about Ann."

Leta knotted her fists at her sides. "Yes, so are we."

Morgan walked to the door and smiled. Leta wanted to snap at him, but she pressed her lips together in a thin, hard line. Morgan said, "Karen! How nice of you to come."

Karen smiled and walked further into the living room.

"I'll leave you two girls alone." Morgan saw the tension between them, but he couldn't understand it. They had been best friends for a long time. He walked to the kitchen for a glass of iced tea.

Karen cleared her throat. "I really am sorry, Leta."

Leta rolled her eyes.

"You're not making this very easy."

"I didn't ask you to come, Karen."

"I know. But we were friends much longer than we were enemies." Karen flushed and held out her hand. "I really didn't mean enemies. You know what I mean."

"I know very well." Leta glanced toward the kitchen. "Morgan doesn't know that we never see each other any more."

"I gathered that much or he wouldn't have left us alone together." Karen flipped back a blond curl. "I really am sorry about Ann."

Leta stepped toward Karen. "Did you take her just to hurt me?"

"Leta! What a terrible thing to say!"

Leta shook her head. "You wouldn't take Ann, would you? You're a pillar of the church. A strong Christian woman who always lends a helping hand. A leader on whom the pastor depends. No, you wouldn't steal Ann. You! You deal with stealing husbands, not children! Don't you?"

Karen's nostrils flared and sparks shot from her blue eyes. "I couldn't take what wasn't half-way out the door."

"Oh, sure."

"I broke it off with Peter. Last month."

Leta stood with her hands at her waist. "Is that supposed to make me feel better? You steal Tracey's husband and break her heart, then brag that Morgan is next!"

"You don't want him, so why shouldn't I have him?"

Leta knotted her fists at her sides. "I do want him and you can't have him."

Karen waved her hand. "We'll see about that. He and I have a date Saturday night."

Leta gasped. Pain exploded inside her. "You're lying!"

"Am I? Call Morgan in here and ask him."

Leta yanked open the door. "Get out, Karen!"

Karen strolled to the door with a small laugh. "You certainly have a temper, Leta."

"I wish I had the nerve to report you to Pastor Ogden!"

"He wouldn't believe you, Leta Hewitt! Not since you practically turned your back on God."

"Because of you, Karen, and you know it!"

"Haven't you learned that you can't look at people? You're supposed to keep your eyes on God. He's perfect; people aren't." She sailed out the door with a wicked chuckle.

Leta slammed the door, anger seething inside her.

Morgan ran into the room. "Leta's, what's wrong?"

"It doesn't matter," she said in a dead voice.

"But it does."

"Forget it, Morgan."

He rattled change in his pockets. "It's Karen, isn't it? Sometimes I don't understand her."

"Oh?"

"She called to see if I had time to go to dinner with her Saturday night." Leta's eyes widened as Morgan continued. "She said she needed to talk to me about a guy she's been seeing. She said they broke up and she needed someone she could trust to talk to. I told her to call you."

Leta laced her trembling fingers together. So, that was the real story! "She doesn't want to talk to me again. And I don't ever want to see her."

"Why?"

"It doesn't matter, Morgan." She turned away from him and stared out the window. "Only Ann matters."

"You're right." He slipped his arms around her and pulled her against him. They stood facing the window and waited.

Amber pushed the photo of Sam Walcott into her purse as she walked wearily to her car. How many times would she have to show the photo before someone recognized him? Her stomach grumbled with hunger and she realized that it was dinnertime and she had missed lunch. Well, it wasn't the first time and it certainly wouldn't be the last.

Traffic roared beside her. The late afternoon sun felt cool against her. The wind had picked up and flipped her skirt and tangled her hair. She glanced up at the sky. Maybe it was going to rain. "April showers bring May flowers," she said as she slid into her car.

. She pulled into traffic and drove slowly toward the highway.

What a day! Maybe she had spent it all in vain. Maybe Sam didn't have Ann. Dr. Grant had been sure of himself, but then the man was only human. He could make a mistake. Amber laughed. He certainly wouldn't admit to a mistake.

Her car phone rang and she grabbed it up. "Yes?"

"Amber, where have you been? I've been trying to reach you!"

It was her secretary. "Carol? What is it?"

"A lead. A good one, Amber."

"Are you still at the office? I can be there in five minutes."

"No, I locked up on time. I wanted to wait, but I have a date tonight with Ricky. You know how long I've waited for him to notice me."

Amber sighed. "That's all right, Carol. What do you have?"

"A man to whom you showed Sam Walcott's picture suddenly remembered that he had seen Walcott working at the Pizza Hut on Britten and Eastern."

Amber stopped at a red light. "You don't say."

"I called your apartment and left the message on your answering machine too."

"Thanks, Carol. Have fun with Randy tonight."

"Ricky."

"Oh, yes. That's right. It was Randy last month."
Carol giggled. "See you in the morning."

"I might not be in before ten."

"There are a couple of people anxious to see you."

"What about?" Amber turned left and stepped on
the gas. She could be at the Pizza Hut in fifteen
minutes.'"Aaron Locklear wants you to see if someone is sabotaging his paint factory and Julie Bennett
wants you to watch her husband to see if he's cheat-
ing on her."

She wrinkled her nose. "I'll talk to them tomorrow." She hung up and wove in and out of traffic.
Just maybe she could find out if Sam Walcott was
her man. She nodded grimly. And if he was, she
would do everything in her power to see that he was
locked up forever. He had no business on the streets.

At Pizza Hut the parking area was almost full, but
she found a spot between a Dodge and a Chevy van.
She trembled. Would she walk inside and find Sam
Walcott?

Amber clutched her purse as she walked toward
the brick building. Pictures of pan pizzas and regular
pizzas made her mouth water. Maybe she should
order a personal pan pizza and eat here instead of
fixing something at home.

She pushed the heavy door open. The aroma of
sauce and meat and spices made her stomach growl.
She stopped at the cash register and waited while the
girl rang up an order, gave the customer his change,
then finally turned to Amber.

"Yes?"

"I'd like to see the manager, please."

The girl hesitated, a funny look on her face. Finally she turned her head and called, "Hey, Cindy,
somebody wants to see you."

A black woman walked from the back and stopped at the counter across from Amber. "What can I do for you?" She shot a look at the cashier. "Is anything wrong?"

Amber held out the picture of Sam Walcott. "I understand this man works here."

Cindy took the picture and studied it with a frown. "No, he doesn't work here."

Amber's heart sank. "Did he ever work here?"

"Yeah, sure, about a month ago." Cindy handed back the picture. "He was strange. Strange. I wanted to make him feel welcome here. We try to be one happy family, you know. I even invited him to my place for a party, but he wouldn't come. He stayed to himself, wouldn't have anything to do with me or the girls. Most guys who work here hit on the girls until they find one that will go with 'em. He wasn't that way."

"Do you know where he works now?"

"Can't say as I do. People come and go, you know. I don't keep track." Cindy leaned forward, her arms on the counter. "He in trouble?"

Amber shrugged. "If you do see him, call me, will you?" She handed Cindy her card.

"Hey! A private detective! Gail, she's a private detective." Cindy puffed up with pride and grinned. "Wait'll I tell my friends that I talked to a real private detective."

Amber smiled and pushed the picture back in her purse. "I'd like a personal pan pizza please, extra cheese, onions, pepperoni. And a 7-UP."

"That'll be five minutes," said Cindy. "I'll bring it to you myself. Five minutes, or you get it free."

Amber walked past a table of high school boys who whistled at her and made smart remarks about her body. She sat at a booth near the window that overlooked her car. She fingered the salt shaker and sighed. She really hadn't expected this job to be easy, had she?

"Hi."

She looked up to find one of the high school boys standing at her table. "Hi. Do you want to talk to me or to my husband the wrestler?" She knew how to handle passes.

The boy shot a look around, his face bright red. "Sorry. I thought you were someone else." He stumbled back to the table and the others roared with laughter.

Cindy slid the pan pizza onto the table, a pleased look on her face. "There you are. I hope you like it."

"Thanks. Mmmm. It smells fabulous!"

"And here's your 7-UP."

"Thanks. Cindy, do you know if Sam Walcott had any friends at all? Did anyone come here to talk to him?"

"No."

"Did he talk about a family?"

Cindy shook her head. "I wish I could help you, but I can't. What'd he do anyway?"

"I can't tell you."

Cindy sighed and her black eyes danced. "This is the most excitement I've had in a long time. I sure would like to be a private eye. I watch TV a lot and I think it would be fun to solve crimes and find lost people. More fun than running this place."

"Someone has to run this place, Cindy." Amber slid a piece of pizza to her plate. Cheese stretched from the pan to the plate and she tugged it apart with her fork. "I do have to eat and run, Cindy. Thanks for your help."

"Any time. Any time." Cindy sashayed across the room to stop at a table of men. Amber could hear her telling them about the private eye eating right here.

Amber turned so she couldn't see them as she chewed the pizza. She should have told Cindy she was working undercover to keep her quiet.

Several minutes later Amber walked outdoors. Wind whipped her long hair across her face. She pulled it back and held it against her slender neck. Just then strong arms grabbed her and lifted her up. She twisted and turned and kicked but he was too strong for her. She could smell beer on his breath and she felt his rough wool jacket. Before she could scream the man clamped a sweaty hand over her mouth and half dragged, half carried her toward a brown Chevy near the dumpster.

Just then a woman called out, "Put her down!"

The man hesitated and Amber's eyes widened as Mina Streebe ran around the back of a car and stopped right in front of the man. Mina's face was as red as her newly dyed hair. The late afternoon sun glinted off her glasses.

"Put her down!" Mina snapped.

"Get away from here," growled the man.

Suddenly Mina leaped behind the man and with the side of her hand she struck a blow to the side of his neck. He grunted and his arms fell away from Amber. She fell to the pavement but leaped up instantly and almost bumped into two people watching. Mina kicked the man with a move that Amber had learned in karate and the man crumpled to the pavement. Mina turned to Amber in concern while the crowd that had gathered cheered.

"Are you all right, Amber?"

Amber stared at Mina. "Are *you* all right?"

"Sure." Mina brushed off Amber's dress. "Oh, my. A rip on the skirt. I might be able to fix that."

Amber shook her head.

The man on the ground groaned.

Mina swooped down on him, her hand out, her fingers against his throat. "Why did you attack this woman?"

The man groaned and looked frightened.

Amber turned to the high school boy who had stopped at her table. "Call the police, will you?"

The boy flushed and grinned. "I already did."

"Thanks." She flashed him a smile before she turned back to Mina and the man. She knelt beside the man. "Talk, mister. You weren't just after my purse."

He swallowed hard. "I heard them say that you were a detective. I thought my wife had hired you. I wanted you to know that I wouldn't stand for being followed."

Amber shook her head impatiently. "I'm not working on a divorce case."

"Don't press charges," he said with a groan. "I don't usually do this kind of thing, but my wife's got me crazy."

Mina stepped back and let the man stand up. "Don't let him off that easy, Amber," Mina said, her eyes narrowed. "I don't trust his face."

Amber hid a grin. "I hear the police now. I'll think about pressing charges and let you know tomorrow."

"Please, lady." The big man bent down to her with his face full of anguish. "I can't spend the night in jail."

Amber crossed her arms and tapped her toe as she studied the man. "All right. We'll just tell the police it was a big misunderstanding."

"Thank you!" The man held out his hand. Amber gave him hers and he pumped it so hard she almost flew into the air.

Mina shook her finger at the man. "It's a good thing you didn't grab me, Mister. I would send you to jail and throw away the key!"

Several minutes later Amber walked to her car with Mina beside her. "Thanks, Mina."

Mina grinned and shrugged a plump shoulder. "Glad to help."

"It was quite a coincidence that you were here." Amber saw the strange look that crossed Mina's face. "Wasn't it?"

Mina cleared her throat. "Don't get mad."

Suspiciously Amber stood beside the car and looked at Mina. "Mad?"

"If I tell you, will you get mad?"

"Stop stalling and tell me!"

Mina picked at her bright red fingernails. "I sort of heard your secretary's message to you."

Amber scowled. "Sort of heard?"

"Don't yell." Mina couldn't bring herself to confess that she'd picked Amber's lock.

"I am not yelling!" Amber knotted her fist at her side. "But I will if you don't talk to me!"

Mina sighed, then squared her shoulders and lifted her chin. "I was in your room and I turned on your answering machine to see if you had anything important on it. I heard about Sam Walcott possibly working here and I decided to drive over and see for myself."

"And just how did you intend to pick him out of the crowd?"

Mina cleared her throat. "I sort of called headquarters and asked for Sheriff Javor. He gave me a description."

Amber threw up her hands. "What am I going to do with you?"

"I saved your life tonight. Remember that, Amber

Ainslie!"

Amber let out her breath. "I suppose you did."

"I just want to help get little Ann Hewitt back."

Amber threw up her hands again, then slapped them at her sides. "You listened to my tape! I should have known someone tampered with my sound system when it blared out this morning."

"I just want to help. And I could if you'd let me."

Amber shook her finger under Mina's nose. "Get out of my sight! I'm too angry to talk to you right now! Get out of here and take your fire-engine red hair with you!"

Mina's face worked and tears filled her eyes. Without a word she walked to her car and drove away.

Amber slammed her car door and sat staring at the fabric store across the parking lot. Her knee stung and she gingerly pulled up her skirt to reveal torn panty hose and a dirty, bloody knee.

She groaned. Even with all her training in self defense she hadn't been able to break away from the man. If Mina hadn't come along, something worse than a bloody knee and ruined panty hose could have happened. Her anger seeped away.

"So, Mina, you want to help me, do you?"

Amber groaned and drove out of the parking lot toward the highway. Suddenly an idea popped into her head. She laughed. Mina could be a big help to her all right! She would ask Mina to help her find a beautiful country home. Then she'd move out of the apartment and far away from her snoopy landlady!

Amber chuckled as she stopped at a red light.

Wanda slipped into her coat and picked up her purse, then turned at a sound behind her. Burl stood just inside the living room, a scowl on his narrow face. Wanda flushed. Without saying a word she rummaged through her purse for her car keys.

Burl folded his thin arms over his thin chest. His mustache moved as he said, "Where do you think you're going?"

"They're having special prayer for Ann at Dolly Hewitt's church tonight. I told her I'd join them."

"Since when do you go to Dolly's church?"

"I'll be back later." She reached for the door, but he caught her arm. She looked at him in surprise.

"Did you ever think to ask if I wanted to go?"

"No. I didn't. Do you want to?"

He thought for a moment, then shook his head.

"Come if you change your mind." With steady steps Wanda walked to her car. When she got home she might tell Burl about her talk with Dolly today, about accepting Christ as her own personal Savior. Wanda nodded. Burl needed the peace and the strength she had found.

She pulled out of the driveway and drove toward church. She wanted to join the others to pray for precious little Ann.

Chapter 10

Dr. Nolen Grant paced his office, nervously stroking his well-trimmed beard. Why couldn't he get Amber Ainslie out of his mind? She had to be wrong about Sam Walcott.

Nolen Grant paced faster. Last night he'd tossed and turned, thinking about what Amber Ainslie had said. He glanced at his desk where the picture of his family had been at one time. His private life was in shambles, but his career was without blemish. He had to keep it that way.

With a low moan he slammed his fist into his palm. Why hadn't he told the detective the truth about Walcott's appointment?

He tapped his appointment book with his finger. If he'd told her that it was today, she would park on his doorstep until she had a chance to talk to Walcott. This way he could double-check his analysis of the patient without any interference from Amber Ainslie.

He glanced at the window to see light rain spatter against it. Soft music played in the background. He dropped to his chair and turned on the recording of his last session with the patient.

Had the patient said something that he missed because of his turmoil over Meg?

Nolen closed his eyes and rubbed his forehead.

Why had she walked out on him after all these years? Why would she be fine for fourteen years, then just walk out without a word? Maybe she had been saying the words and he simply hadn't heard them.

His recorded voice interrupted his thoughts and he turned his attention to the tape.

"Sam, you talked about cooking last time and how you like it. Shall we start there today?"

"I learned to cook in prison. I like to cook."

Discussion of cooking in general followed. Nolen narrowed his eyes as he remembered how agitated Sam had become over a meatloaf he'd made.

"I like to make meatloaf." Sam used the index finger on his right hand to rub between the fingers on his left hand. He perched on the edge of his chair, his back stiff, perspiration dotting his forehead. "I made a meatloaf last night. When it was cooked almost all the way through, I took it out of the oven and dug a hole in the middle with a spoon." He rubbed his finger harder between his other fingers. "I stuck the spoon in and pulled out the meat. Finally I had a perfect hole. I took little green peas and I dropped them one by one into the perfect hole. One at a time." He licked his lips, leaving them moist. "I worked on filling the hole until it was full. Some say it's dumb to do that. They think I should use my time doing something different." He licked his lips again. "My sisters tease me because I'm not married." He jumped up. "Momma used to check my pants pockets to see what I had in them. She still does that sometimes and I don't like it."

"You don't like it?"

"I'm not a little boy any more. It's not her business what I have in my pocket." He had grown very agitated, then changed the subject to his job as a cook at Pizza Hut.

Nolen Grant clicked off the tape, leaned his elbows on his desk and cupped his face in his hands. Sam didn't realize that he had revealed his sexual stress. That stress was caused by his family background.

With a sigh Nolen clicked in another tape. It was rainy the day of this taping, much like today. Sam had removed his cap and shook off the rain.

"I hate the rain."

"Why do you think you dislike being wet?"

"I don't know. I always have." He walked around the room, then finally sat on the chair that he always chose.

"When was the first time you can remember being wet and disliking it?"

Sam gripped the arms of his chair and angry sparks shot from his eyes. "I hated taking a bath when I was a kid."

"Hated a bath?"

"My sisters watched and they wouldn't leave when Momma washed me. They laughed at me."

"Laughed?"

"I wasn't made like them and they laughed. I couldn't help it that I wasn't made like them."

He told about his sisters giving him baths, touching him and teasing him about his difference.

"They laughed and laughed at me. I didn't want them to. I didn't want anyone to laugh. I never took showers in school 'cause the kids laughed at me. Big kids laughed, but little girls liked me." He licked his lips and ran his finger around the circle of his mouth. "They liked me. But that was when I was younger."

"When you were younger?"

"Yes. And not now I guess. There were those

times I did something really bad and got put in jail. I could never hurt little girls like that again.

He jumped up and changed the subject. Nolen clicked off the tape and walked nervously around the room. Would a man with such a deep-rooted problem be able to stay away from little girls? He had to get sexual relief somewhere and he was afraid of women. Nolen tugged at his beard.

What if Sam did have the little girl that Amber Ainslie had told him about?

The phone buzzed and he picked it up. He listened as Marlene told him that Sam Walcott had arrived. "Send him in, Marlene."

Nolen clicked in a new tape and walked around to meet Sam. Maybe today he could learn if Sam had abducted a little girl. Nolen's muscles knotted and he forced a smile on his face for Sam. "Hello. Rainy day today."

Sam nodded and walked restlessly around the room. His brown hair was combed neatly and his beard and mustache trimmed carefully. He had almost cancelled his appointment for fear of spilling his secret about Ann, but he knew it was a stipulation of his parole. He would be very, very careful what he said. Dr. Grant must never guess about Ann.

Nolen walked around his desk, sat down and studied Sam carefully. "We were talking about the sexual pleasure young girls give you."

Sam stiffened. "I didn't say that!"

"Didn't you?"

Sam dropped to his chair, his breathing suddenly ragged. "Maybe I did say it."

As they talked Sam's palms, forehead and armpits dampened with perspiration.

"Sam, do you think all men feel the same as you do toward young girls?"

Sam thought about that for a long time and carefully considered his answer. "I guess they don't. I guess I would rather be like other men. I don't like to be different."

"You would rather not be different."

"Maybe I could test myself to see if I could be around a little girl and not touch her or rub against her; not do anything to her but talk and look at her. Maybe I could test myself that way."

Nolen's heart almost jumped through his suit jacket, but he kept a bland look on his face. "Test yourself."

Sam felt very secure, very safe. No doctor could ever see through him! "I could find a little girl, maybe take her home, and then maybe just look at her and maybe talk to her."

"Take her home?" Nolen fought to keep his voice level, his face free of his horror.

"I could do it just to see if I would do anything bad to her."

"Bad?"

"You know. Like I did before. Before jail." He rubbed his index finger between the fingers of his other hand. "I would never hurt a little girl like that again. I want little girls to like me."

"Like you?"

"Yes. If they like me they won't care if I touch them or anything." He moistened his lips. "They'll like it. I can do anything I want."

"Anything you want?" A shiver ran down Nolen's spine as he realized that Sam did indeed have a girl at his place.

Sam lifted his head, suddenly alert to tension in the air. "I mean if I wanted, but I don't want little girls any longer. I want to be like you, like other men."

"And go with women instead of girls."

"Women that wouldn't laugh at me." Sam pushed himself up and stood at the window watching the rain splatter against the sidewalk. Would Dr. Grant guess about Ann? Sam shook his head slightly. He hadn't said anything to give himself away. He didn't have anything to worry about. He turned around with a small smile.

Nolen leaned back in his chair in a way he hoped looked relaxed and natural. "How do you like your new home?"

Sam stiffened. "What new home?"

"Don't you remember? You mentioned it last visit."

Sam frantically searched his brain. What had he said last visit? He couldn't remember. "I like it all right."

"That's good. Is it close enough to where you work so you can walk?"

"It is but I drive. Thirty hours a week I work, but it pays the rent."

"Tell me about your place." Nolen felt as if he'd jump right out of his skin, but he kept a small smile on his face.

"It's a duplex with one bedroom." He thought of Ann curled up on his bed and he skittered away from that. "And a nice kitchen where I can cook anything I want."

"Do your mother and sisters visit you?"

"They don't know about my new job. Or my new place. I don't want them to visit me and laugh at me."

"Laugh at you?"

"Bonnie always wants to know if I have a girl-friend. Jannie says no woman would want me, ever. She says only little girls would. I said she shouldn't

have taught me to play with little girls and she says
I've shamed them all. Momma told them not to be
mean to me because I'm their little brother no matter
what I did."

"Were you glad she said that?"

"No! She makes fun of me just like Bonnie and
Jannie. She even said I should be big enough by now
to handle big girls. And then she laughed." Sam
pounded the desk twice. "If I want little girls, then
I'll take them. I can take a little girl and never touch
her. I can do that. I know I can."

"How do you know?"

"Because I'm better than I was before. I won't hurt
another little girl ever."

"Not ever?"

"Never! I can stop myself. I couldn't before, but I
can this time. This time."

Nolen slowly leaned forward. How he wanted to
grab Sam and shake his new address out of him so
he could save the child! He knew he had to be very
careful or he'd scare Walcott into silence. "What did
you cook at work today, Sam?"

"French fries."

"Is that all?"

"I'm in charge of them."

"Did you eat any of them?"

Sam nodded.

"What else?"

"A Whopper."

Nolen's pulse raced. "Would you make a Whopper
for me if I stop in?"

"I could make you fries."

"That's fine. What Burger King is it? I'll stop in
today or tomorrow for sure." Had he sounded a little
too eager?

Sam opened his mouth to answer Dr. Grant, then

snapped it closed. He didn't want anyone to find out about his needing a shrink. They might fire him. If he didn't have a job he wouldn't be able to keep his new apartment. And without that place he couldn't keep Ann safe and happy. "I'll bring you a Whopper next time I come talk to you, Dr. Grant. That would be better."

Nolen's heart dropped to his well-polished black shoes. "Fine. I'll like that."

"Is it time for me to leave now?"

"Are you in a hurry today?"

"No. Oh, no! I just thought it was time." He wanted to get back to Ann. Today he would help her brush her hair. That's all he'd do, brush her long, beautiful, blond hair. He wouldn't do anything else to her.

Nolen slowly stood. "You run along if you want, Sam. We'll talk again Monday."

Sam nodded.

Nolen smiled his gentle smile as Sam walked out and closed the door. The smile faded and perspiration soaked his forehead. He dashed across the room, his face red. He'd been wrong. Wrong! What would happen to his career if this ever hit the papers? It was sure to do so if he called Amber Ainslie and she in turn told the police.

He groaned. Could he handle a mark against his spotless career?

But what of the little girl?

He ran to his desk and frantically searched the top of his desk for Amber Ainslie's card. He jerked open his top middle drawer and rummaged through it. Finally he found the card under a few paper clips. His hand trembled as he lifted the receiver and dialed the number.

"Ainslie Detective Agency."

"Amber Ainslie, please."

"I'm sorry. She's out of the office. May I take a message and have her get back with you?"

He ground his teeth. "Tell her Dr. Nolen Grant called. Tell her I have information on Sam Walcott."

Carol sucked in her breath. She knew Amber would want the information immediately. "Please leave your number and Amber will call you ASAP."

He barked out his number and then turned away from the phone as if it would bite him.

Just how long would it take Amber Ainslie to call him? He might be gone for the day and then what would she do? No way would he give out his home number.

He pulled his white handkerchief from his breast pocket and mopped his brow. Well, he did his part. What more was expected of him? It wasn't his fault that Sam Walcott hadn't responded to therapy.

Nolen breathed deeply, straightened his tie, brushed his hair back in place, then sat down to wait for his next patient.

Chapter 11

For the hundredth time Leta looked at the kitchen clock as she paced from the kitchen to the living room to the bedrooms and back. The silence of the house oppressed her. Morgan wanted to stay home again today but he couldn't afford to lose his job at Queens. She promised to call him if she heard any news about Ann.

"The third day," cried Leta, stopping in front of the calendar that hung beside the bedroom telephone. "She's been gone two days and today. It seems like a year."

Rain spattered the windows. Usually she enjoyed spring rains but today the rain depressed her.

The phone rang and the muscles in her neck tightened until her head ached. She grabbed the phone and cried, "Hello."

"Mrs. Hewitt?"

The voice was whiny and Leta couldn't tell if it was a man or woman. "Yes?"

"I got your little girl."

"What?" Leta pressed her hand against her soft yellow sweater over her heart. "Who are you? Where are you?"

"If you yell at me, I won't tell you."

Leta breathed deeply and forced herself to calm down. "Tell me who you are."

"She's here with me. I got her right here. Little blond girl with a pink blouse on. Blue eyes."

"Yes, yes. That's her."

"Ann's her name and she's nine."

"Yes!" Leta struggled to catch her breath.

"You want her back?"

"Don't do this to me. Of course I want her back! Tell me where she is and I'll come get her."

"You bring me money and she's yours."

"Money? I don't have any."

"I'm not askin' for much, you understand. Only five thousand. Five thousand and she's yours."

Frantically Leta searched her mind for a way to get the money. Ann's savings account that her grandparents had started when Ann was born! "Just tell me where I can find Ann."

"You bring the money."

Blood pounded in her ears. "I will. I will! Tell me where!"

Outside a siren wailed. Leta jumped and almost dropped the phone.

"Bring the money to the park and I'll find you. Sit on the bench near the wishing well. And don't tell the cops or I'll know and you'll never see your little girl again."

"The park. Near the wishing well."

"Five thousand dollars. In one hour." The person hung up and the dial tone buzzed in Leta's ear.

She glanced at her watch. "Ten. By eleven I have to be at the park. Ann will be there and I'll get her back."

Tears ran down her face as she jerked open the desk drawer and fumbled through the file for Ann's savings account book.

At the bank the teller seemed to take forever to count out the money. Leta stood on first one foot, then the other. Was Ann waiting out in the rain at the park?

Leta snatched up the money and turned right into Sheriff Fritz Javor's powerful arms.

"What's going on here?" he asked softly.

She pushed against him, but he felt like a brick wall. "I'm going after Ann. I have to give them the money and they'll give me Ann."

"They?" Fritz's gut hurt for the woman, but he couldn't let her fall for such an obvious trap. He had told the people at the bank to call him if either of the Hewitts came in to withdraw a large sum of money. As she babbled on he led her to a secluded spot behind two green plants. He tried to cut in, but she wouldn't stop talking. Again she tried to push past him, but he held her firmly.

"Why are you doing this to me? Let me go! I have to get Ann!"

"Mrs. Hewitt. Leta. Simmer down. It's a trick. Only a cruel trick."

She shook her head and whimpered.

He tightened his arm around her. She could smell smoke on his uniform and coffee on his breath. "Leta, let us handle this. You can't take money to the person in the park."

"What about Ann?"

"She's probably not there. But we'll look for her. Don't you worry."

"I won't go back home! I want to go to the park with you." Her face crumpled and she pressed her hand against his chest. "Please. Please, I have to."

Fritz sighed, then nodded. He wouldn't go home if it was his kid. "You can come, but you stay with me. Right at my side. Hear me?"

She nodded.

"I'll have a policewoman go in your place. One

with the same brown hair and build." He patted the hand that gripped the money. "You put that back and then we'll go."

A giant tear rolled down her ashen cheek. Slowly she walked with him to the teller and deposited the money in Ann's account.

He led her to his unmarked car. "Did you call Amber Ainslie about the call?"

"I didn't think of it."

"She might've wanted to check it out herself. She's a good detective. Let her do her job, will you?" He saw the tears slide silently down Leta's cheeks and he bit back any further lecture. She was hurting enough without adding to it.

At the park he pulled up near the tennis court. "We're going to slip through those trees and get close. I don't want you to say a word or we just might lose this guy. Not one word, you hear?"

She nodded.

He didn't want her with him, but it was better to have her where he could keep an eye on her. "Missy Harris, the police officer, will be here soon. She'll sit on that bench and we'll watch. She'll be dressed in slacks and a sweater like you. Her hair is darker than yours but I don't think it'll matter."

"Do you think Ann is here somewhere?"

"I don't think so, but I got people looking just in case." He slipped out into the light rain while Leta slid out the passenger door.

The rain dampened Leta's sweater and slacks and frizzled her hair. She looked around, but couldn't see another person from where she stood.

Fritz took her hand and together they crept through the trees. He stopped behind a clump of bushes where they could easily see the bench beside the wishing well. He felt Leta shudder as Missy

Harris ran to the bench and perched on the edge as if she was too tense to sit back.

A small man wearing a gray hat and an all-weather brown jacket crept out from bushes behind the bench. Missy Harris heard him and leaped up turning just the way Leta knew she would do.

"You got the money?" the man asked.

"Where's my baby? Where's Ann?" Missy sounded as frantic as Leta would if she were facing the man.

"Give me the money and I'll tell you where she is." The man lunged at Missy and she let him grab her purse and run. She waited about five seconds, then raced after the man. With a flying leap she tackled him, knocking him to the ground with a thud.

Leta suddenly knew Ann wasn't in the park. "He lied to me. Ann's not here at all." Leta turned her face into Fritz's chest and sobbed.

Tears burned his eyes as he held her. When he got home today he would call Bruce and talk to him, maybe set up a fishing date with him. Fathers and sons had no business living apart.

Later at home Leta walked into her bathroom in a daze. Fritz had told her to go home, take a hot shower and go to bed for a while.

Slowly she dropped her wet clothes in a heap on the tile floor and stepped into the steaming shower.

The bright yellow umbrella over her head, Amber dashed through the rain to her office. What a miserable day to do legwork. She dropped the wet umbrella to the right of the door and pulled off her jacket. "Anything new, Carol?" Carol was short and slender with dark hair and gray eyes. She looked up from the letter she was reading.

"Dr. Nolen Grant called."

Amber's heart lurched. "When?"

"At eleven."

"Why didn't you call me?"

"I tried. Several times."

Amber ran to her office, shouting, "Get him on the line for me, Carol." She knew he wouldn't call unless it was important. She dropped to her chair and reached for the phone. Was it already too late to reach him?

"He's on the line," called Carol.

"Amber Ainslie here, Dr. Grant. I'm sorry I missed your call."

He tugged at his beard. "You almost didn't catch me. I was on my way out." It still wasn't too late to keep the information about Walcott to himself.

Amber pressed her toes into the carpet. "Do you have information for me, Dr. Grant?"

"Have you found the child?"

"No. Did you get Sam Walcott's new address?"

"No." Nolen cleared his throat. "I had a session with him today."

"Today!" Amber shot from her chair, her eyes flashing. "And you didn't tell me?"

"I didn't find it necessary."

"What?" She grabbed a handful of her red hair and pulled. She wanted to rant and rave at him, but knew he would hang up. Taking a deep breath, she said gently, "What did you learn during your talk?"

"I believe he has a child."

"Oh, dear God." Amber sank weakly to her chair. "Ann?"

"I don't know."

"And?"

"I tried to get his new address, but he caught on and wouldn't tell me. I did learn that he works at a

Burger King within walking distance of his place. A duplex."

"That helps. Anything else?"

He fingered his beard. "The girl isn't in danger at this time. But he could lose control. Then there would be danger to the child." He closed his eyes. "I hope you find her."

"Thank you, Dr. Grant. You have helped and I really appreciate it. If you learn anything more, let me know."

"I will." He hesitated. "Miss Ainslie."

"Yes."

"Will you call me when you find the child?"

"Yes."

"Thank you."

"I don't have your home number."

"I know. Call me at the office." He hung up and leaned back with a weary sigh. She said he had helped and she appreciated it. A warm feeling spread through him and he actually smiled.

Amber sat at her computer getting information on Burger King employees. Maybe they'd have Sam Walcott's new address—if he gave his real name.

Her neck muscles ached as she read down the employee list. Suddenly Sam Walcott's name leaped off the screen at her and she shouted in triumph, then her smile faded. His home address was the same one she had. But she had new information now. She scribbled the address of the Burger King. If he worked dinner shift, he would still be there. If he didn't, she could learn something about him.

Amber kicked off her damp heels and pulled jeans and a sweater from her coat closet. She always tried to keep a change of clothes on hand. She slipped out of her dress and into the jeans and sweater. She pushed her feet into soft loafers and felt ready for anything. At Carol's desk she stopped and explained what she had learned and where she would be.

Carol smiled. "You call me if you find Ann."

"I will."

"I'll be home all evening."

"No date tonight?"

Carol wrinkled her nose. "Only with the TV."

"Pray for Ann. And for me. Dr. Grant says Walcott's going to break. Ann or not, I'll get that girl from him and send Walcott away for a long, long time.

"Should I call Fritz Javor?"

"No. I will later." Amber ran through the rain to her car and slipped inside. Wouldn't she love it if she could call Fritz and tell him that she had Ann safe and sound!

At Burger King she parked beside a blue Ford. Butterflies fluttered in her stomach and she took several deep breaths to steady herself.

Was Sam Walcott working inside right now?

She walked inside. It was almost empty but full of smells of fries, hamburgers and onions. She walked to the door marked 'for employees only'. Before she could push it open a tall woman in her fifties stopped her.

"May I help you?"

"I'm looking for a man who works here. I have important business with him."

"I'm sorry, but you can't go back there." The woman planted herself firmly in front of the door with her arms crossed over her heavy bosom.

Amber thought about showing her badge, then changed her mind. She didn't want to alert Sam Walcott. She smiled and shrugged. "I guess it can wait."

"Who did you want?"

"Sam Walcott. Is he here now?"

"Yes, but he's on a break. I'll find him and send him out."

Amber shook her head. "I want to surprise him. I'll wait until he's off work and then I'll see him." She leaned toward the woman as if she was going to tell her a secret. "You won't give me away, will you?"

The woman's face softened and she almost smiled. "I'm too busy to get involved. He gets off in about an hour."

Amber ordered a fish sandwich and ice water. She sat in a booth away from the other customers and ate in silence. Later she walked to her car and waited for Sam. Her phone rang and she jumped so hard she bumped her arm on the door.

"Amber here," she said.

"It's Mina, Amber. I thought you'd be home by now."

Amber frowned. "What's up, Mina?"

"You got an important call. Now, don't get mad at me again. I know I promised to stay out of your place, but I heard your phone ringing off the hook. I had to see if it was important to the Hewitt case."

"So, what is it, Mina?" Tomorrow she'd change the locks again, or get a vicious dog.

"Morgan Hewitt called. He said the police near Grand Rapids found a body with Ann's general description and they have to go to the morgue and ID it. He wants you to meet them there."

"I can't, Mina. I'm onto something that I can't leave."

"Morgan Hewitt sounded desperate."

Amber drummed her fingers on the steering wheel, then smiled wickedly. "Mina, I hate to ask you, but could you go to the morgue for me?"

"Oh, Amber! Are you serious?"

"Sure. But the morgue's not your usual Sunday School party."

"I know. I'll go with them and report back to you."

"I don't know when I'll be back." Amber watched a young couple walk arm in arm out of the Burger King.

"The police found the body in a field just outside of Freburg. Mr. Hewitt's trying real hard to believe that it's not Ann.

"I'd rather believe she's alive and that we'll find her soon."

"I know what you mean."

Amber hung up and leaned back just as the outside lights flashed on. Was the body in the morgue Ann Hewitt? "Dear God, don't let it be," she breathed.

Just then the back door opened and Sam Walcott walked out. His uniform fit him nicely and he had a pleasant look on his face. In one hand he carried a white Burger King bag and in the other hand, his cap. He didn't look like he could molest a child.

He walked to his gray and black Chevy and drove out without a look around.

Amber ground her teeth. How could the man be so sure of himself? She started her car and followed him. From Broadmoor he turned on Hickory. He stopped at a red light and she pulled up right behind him. If she wanted to she could ram right into his bumper.

The rain stopped and she rolled down her window and let in the cool breeze. Cars and trucks drove through the intersection, their tires noisy on the wet pavement. The light turned and Sam drove through. Before Amber could move ahead, a car slammed into her rear end. She pitched forward, but her seat belt caught and held her. Helplessly she watched Sam's taillights fade away in the distance.

Trembling, she gripped the steering wheel. Immediately a policeman bent down to her window.

"You all right, miss?"

"Yes, but I don't have time to report this right now."

"Your taillights are out. You're not going anywhere."

Impatiently she gave insurance information, then drove to the Buick garage just a block away and parked near the used cars.

"Heavenly Father, whether it is Ann or not, keep that little girl safe from Walcott. And help me get her away from him."

She dialed Fritz Javor and let the phone ring and ring. And ring. On the tenth ring he answered and her eyes pricked with sudden tears.

"Fritz, I need you."

"You caught me in the shower, Red. What's up?"

She told him in short, quick sentences. "Dr. Grant said that he lives within walking distance of his workplace. I know his car. We could drive around and find his car. Then I could get the girl."

"We can't go looking in every garage."

"Few places in this neighborhood have garages." Amber leaned her head against the car window. "Do you want to come drive me around or should I call someone else?"

"Come on, Red."

"I was so close!"

"I know. I'll be there in twenty-five minutes."

She sat up straight. "Make it fifteen."

"You want me to break the law?" He chuckled and she grinned.

Chapter 12

They stepped into the silent living room. Leta turned to Morgan's strong arms.

"Thank God! Thank God, it wasn't Ann," she cried into his chest. His heart hammered against her ear. She clung to him as she thought of the horrible experience in the morgue.

The girl had been larger than Ann with short hair and a tiny scar under her chin. By the time they left, someone had identified her as Margaret Brodie from Lansing; missing since January fifteenth.

Leta pressed tightly against Morgan. What if they didn't find Ann for months and then were called to identify her body at the morgue? Leta shivered and Morgan led her to the couch. They sat huddled together, drawing strength from being near each other. Finally she lifted her haggard face. "Will you stay again tonight, Morgan? You won't leave me alone, will you?"

He wiped a tear from her pale cheek and his hazel eyes softened. Dare he suggest that he move back in for good? He reached for the courage and found it. "I want to come home, Leta, if you'll have me."

Her heart leaped.

"You do? Are you sure?"

He nodded. "I want to be the husband and father I should've been all along."

It wasn't just that simple. She had to settle it, to know for sure.

She looked down at their clasped hands, then into his face. "What about . . . about Karen?"

"What about her?"

Leta wanted to grab the words back, then decided to get it all out in the open. Why should she let Karen Blackley ruin one more day of her life? "She said you have a date Saturday night."

"It was only dinner. She'll be glad to see us back together."

Leta jumped up and faced Morgan with her fists clenched at her sides. The ticking clock on the small table kept time with her heartbeats. "I'll tell you about Karen Blackley"

"What about her?"

"She steals husbands!"

"Karen?"

"Don't looked so shocked. She took Peter! And last year she stole Abe and before him was Thomas."

"No!"

"Think about it, Morgan."

"But she's not that kind of person."

"That's what I thought but I was wrong." Leta tossed back her honey brown hair. "She says she's a Christian. That's an awful way for a Christian to act."

Morgan slowly reached for Leta and she let him draw her back beside him. "You can't let Karen keep you from God."

She froze.

"I don't want anything to do with Christians if they act like Karen."

"You know they don't." He smoothed back her hair. "Jesus is perfect. We are supposed to look at His life and follow His example."

Leta's lip quivered. Was it really so simple? "It's so hard."

"No, it isn't. But we need each other to make it easier. I haven't been any help to you. I grew cold toward God and that made me cold toward you. When things got tough between us we had no strength to fight it. Don't you see what happened to us?"

"What?" she whispered.

"We allowed the devil to come in and try to destroy us. You know his job is to kill, steal and destroy. We *let* him destroy our marriage. But no longer! From this moment on we're going to read the Bible and follow what we read. We're going to pray together. We're going to do what *God* wants us to do."

"Oh, Morgan. I feel so empty inside."

He pulled her close. "Let's pray together. For us. And for Ann."

Leta nodded.

After they prayed Morgan said, "There is one more thing we must do, Leta."

"I know what I must do," said Leta, her face set with determination. "But it's not going to be easy."

"What?"

She smoothed his shirt absently as she looked into his face. "Karen has caused enough pain in the church. Since I know what she's doing, it's up to me to stop her."

"What will you do?"

"I'll . . . I'll warn Karen to stop her wrongdoing." Leta clung to Morgan's hand. "And if she won't, I'll tell Pastor Ogden what she's doing so he will take away her church responsibilities. I will not let Karen make another person stop trusting God!"

"That will take a lot of courage, Leta."

"I know. But I can't do *nothing*. Not any more, I can't!"

"I know." Morgan gently held her face in his hands and kissed her trembling lips. He pulled back and said, "There is one more thing we must do."

"What?"

He took a deep, ragged breath. "While we prayed God spoke to my heart about it."

Leta lifted a fine brow.

"It's Sally Perrin."

Leta pulled away. "What about her?" she asked coldly.

"We must forgive her."

"What? How can we? Look what she did to us!"

"You know that Jesus says we are to forgive others. If we let anger and bitterness toward Sally come between us and God it blocks our fellowship with Him. It also leaves room in our lives for Satan to attack. We don't want that, do we?"

Leta bit her lip and finally said, "You're right. Oh, but it's hard!"

"Jesus will help us. With His strength we can forgive Sally. And we won't hold it against her."

"Oh, Morgan!"

"With God's help I forgive Sally," said Morgan.

Leta hung her head. "I can't do it."

"Yes, you can."

"It's too hard."

"With God's help you can." Morgan stroked her arm. "You don't have a choice, Leta. Jesus said that we *must* forgive others."

Leta closed her eyes and moaned. Finally she whispered, "I forgive Sally. Please help me, Father God! And bring our little Ann safely home to us."

The clock on the table beside the front door chimed.

"It's twelve already," said Morgan in surprise.

"Day four starts," whispered Leta. "Oh, I want Ann home in her own bed. I want to see her play with her teddy bears. I want to take her shopping."

"I want to tell her we're a family again," said Morgan with a crack in his voice.

Wanda Stanley slid out of bed. Burl flipped on his side and snored louder. Wanda pulled on her robe and pushed her bare feet into soft slippers. Inside she felt a peace that she knew came from God.

In the living room she clicked on the reading lamp and curled up in her chair with a Bible in her hand. She quietly read aloud Psalm 91. Dolly had said that Psalm was a great comfort.

"Reading that again?" asked Burl gruffly.

She looked up to see him belting his robe around his stick-thin body. "I could read it to you if you want."

"What good would it do?" He sank to the couch. Her peaceful attitude made him envious. In all his years he'd never had peace of heart or mind. Could religion make the difference after all?

"The Bible is God's words for us today, Burl. You know that."

"Religion." He scowled and his bushy brows met over his huge nose.

"No, Burl. Not religion at all. It's a personal relationship with God, the Creator. He knows you by your name. He loves you. You are important to Him."

He felt like a drowning man reaching for a life preserver.

She read Psalm 103 to him and then they sat in silence.

Finally he said, "Wanda, I do care for our children."

"Oh, Burl!"

"I just never knew how to show it."

"I'm sorry about that. You missed out on a lot."

"I know."

"And I'm sorry about our baby girl."

Wanda bit her lip.

He cleared his throat. "I've just now decided that I need a change in my life. I need to talk to Morgan and Leta and tell them to stay together." His voice broke. "Ann. Our little Ann. She understood me without my saying the words."

"You mean she knew that you loved her?"

"Yes." He brushed a hand across his eyes. "How can we survive without her? She was sunshine in this house."

"I know." Wanda stood and slowly walked to the couch.

He watched her, his heart in his mouth.

She sat beside him, wrapped her arms around him and held him close to her. "Burl, we can learn to love each other with God's help. I need you. You need me too."

Tears filled his eyes and flowed down his cheeks. He caught Wanda to him and held her tight.

Amber spotted Fritz as he turned onto the street. In a flash she slipped from her car, locked it and ran to his dark blue Pontiac.

"Hi." He smiled as she slid into the passenger seat. She smelled chocolate and saw the empty candy bar wrapper on the floor.

"Thanks for coming, Fritz."

"I'm glad to see you didn't start off on foot."

"I thought about it, believe me. You know waiting is hard work." She told him the route to take and he drove to the residential area.

"I put out the description of Walcott's car, so everyone patrolling tonight is looking for it. I couldn't order the police here in Freburg to do anything, but they're cooperating with me. For that I'm glad." He could feel her tension as they slowly drove down Maple Street. He wanted to say something to help ease the tension, but he couldn't find the words. "You're getting too involved with this, Red."

She shot a sharp look at him. "I know. But I can't help it."

"Is it because of Morgan Hewitt?" Jealousy rose inside him surprising him. Impatiently he forced it away.

"Maybe." She blinked fast to hold back tears. "But mostly it's that little girl. We know Walcott has a girl. Maybe it's not Ann. We might find Walcott tonight but might not find Ann. That means we keep looking. It's been a long day."

"I know, Red."

"Do you know you're the only person that I allow to call me Red?"

That pleased him. "You don't say?"

"Wait!" She grabbed his arm and he slowed to a crawl. "I think I saw the car. Back a couple of houses!"

He looked around, saw that the street was clear and slowly backed up. "It's not a Chevy."

Her heart sank. "It's not. All the black and gray cars are beginning to look alike."

"We could pack it in and start fresh in the morning."

She shook her head. "I can't. But if you want to, you can. I have to find Walcott. I have to find that little girl!"

"We'll both keep going."

"Thanks."

A truck with his bright lights on drove toward them and blinded Amber for a moment. She blinked to get rid of the black dots and circles. A dog ran out and barked at their tires.

Fritz reached over and squeezed her hand. She relaxed slightly.

Amber smiled at him. "Did anyone ever tell you that you're pretty wonderful?"

"Yah, a lot of folks." Her words warmed him but he didn't let it show.

"Sure, I bet all of them were women," she said sharply.

"Jealous?" He forced a light laugh.

Suddenly she leaned forward and peered out the windshield. "That's it, Fritz! That's the car!" Shivers ran over her and she shook her finger at the car. "Am I right? Is it a Chevy?"

"It's a Chevy." He pulled up behind the car and studied the surroundings. "Let me call in the plates and see if we have the right car."

She sat on her icy hands and waited while he used the CB to call. Did Sam Walcott live in the dark house to her right? She looked back at the car. "Why didn't I get the license number before?" she muttered. Her eyes widened. "His car had mud on the plate. I couldn't read the number. That plate is clean."

"Maybe he washed it."

"Or maybe it's not his."

He tugged one of her red curls. "It won't hurt to wait another minute and get a report."

"I guess." She twisted in the seat and looked around at the neighborhood. Something Dr. Grant had said seemed important to remember. What was it?

Fritz squeezed the back of her neck with a big, strong hand. "Relax, Amber."

Just then a voice spoke on the CB and gave information about the owner of the Chevy. It wasn't Sam Walcott.

Fritz pulled away from the curb and continued down the street. Most of the houses were dark for the night. Only an occasional car drove past.

Amber cleared her throat. "Dr. Grant said Walcott was trying to test himself and not touch the girl. But he might break. We just can't be too late, Fritz!"

"Keep the faith, Red."

She nodded. "Yes. Yes, I will!" She pushed red curls out of her face and peered out the window.

Chapter 13

Ann opened her eyes, sat up in bed and looked around the dimly lit bedroom. The terror she'd lived with was gone. In its place was a quiet determination to get away from Sam, away from his constant demand that they be great friends. He said he loved her and wouldn't hurt her but he wouldn't let her go home. She knew he didn't really love her. When he was leaving for work he would chain her to the bed with a chain long enough to reach the bathroom. When he was home he set her free and watched her every move. No matter what he said she knew she was a prisoner.

She dressed quietly in her only clothes, jeans, her pink blouse and sneakers. Her clothes smelled dirty but she didn't care. She was going home. But first she had to get her bear. Her heart raced as she lifted the covers and looked under them. The bear wasn't there. She peeked under the bed. The bear was small enough to fit in her jacket pocket and she had kept it a secret from Sam. She knew he would take it from her. Finally she found the bear, kissed it, and held it in her hand for courage. She tiptoed to the door, her arms out to balance herself.

Sam slept on the couch. She heard his soft breathing. Was he really asleep or was he only pretending so that he could grab her if she walked past him?

She shivered, but crept forward.

The floor creaked and she stopped, her eyes wide. Could he hear her breathing? Could he hear how loud her heart was beating?

The street light shone softly into the room. She could see his outline on the couch, the cover half on and half off. A bowl containing a few kernels of popcorn sat on the floor. Last night he had popped corn. She ate a little bit just to keep him from yelling at her. The smell of popcorn and Sam's sweat hung in the air. She wrinkled her nose.

Ann crept to the kitchen door. The front door in the living room was blocked by a bookcase that held four books, a few odd-shaped rocks and some model cars. He had told her all about building the cars and finding the rocks.

In the kitchen she reached for the dead-bolt lock. She wasn't strong enough to unlock it. Setting her bear on the table near the salt shaker, Ann reached for the lock with both hands. It turned with a squawk. She held her breath, listening for sounds from Sam. None came so she slowly, carefully opened the door. Chilly wind blew against her and she shivered. She started to step out, then remembered the bear. She couldn't leave her bear to become Sam's prisoner.

Ann swallowed hard then took the two steps to the table and picked up her bear. She stepped back to the door and slowly, carefully pushed open the screen. If she could run down the two steps, past the car and into the street, she could get away. The screen squeaked and she froze.

Suddenly Sam grabbed her arm and hauled her back away from the door. She screamed and he slammed the door. "You can't run away from me, Ann! We're friends forever!"

She trembled as she looked up at him. He wore baggy striped pajamas. His hair stood on end. His feet were bare. "I want to go home!" she cried. "We are not friends!"

"Don't say that! Don't!" He pulled her close and held her tightly against him. "I can't lose you now."

She smelled his perspiration and bad breath. She struggled and finally he let her go. She ran behind a kitchen chair and stared at him with wide frightened eyes. "Are you gonna kill me?"

"Kill you? Oh, I would never kill you, Ann. I love you!" He stepped toward her and she cringed back, keeping the chair between them.

He shook his finger at her. "I've been good to you, Ann. I didn't hurt you like I did the other girls. I said I could keep you here and not hurt you, and I will do it. I mean it."

"Please let me go home. I want my mom and dad."

"But I need you, Ann." He caught her arm and she squealed and dropped her bear.

He didn't see it and she didn't want to draw attention to it. He might kill her bear.

He pushed her onto the chair. "You sit right there. It's almost time for breakfast. We'll sit here and eat and talk and maybe I'll tell you a joke."

She rubbed her eyes and sniffled.

He reached out to stroke her hair, then jerked his hand back. He wouldn't do that. Suddenly he smiled. He had been good for so long he really did deserve a reward. After breakfast he would sit on the couch and hold Ann on his lap. He nodded. That would be his reward. And he deserved it.

Amber nodded off to sleep, then jerked awake. "Did I miss a Chevy, Fritz?"

"No, Amber. Go ahead and grab a little sleep. I'll watch by myself."

She rolled down the window and refreshing cool air blew against her face. "I can't let you watch alone. What street are we on?"

"Pine."

She glanced at his gas gauge. "You're almost on empty."

"I know. I thought we'd go a while longer, then stop for gas and a bite of breakfast. I'm hungry. What about you?"

She shrugged. Her stomach growled and she laughed. "I guess I am hungry."

Fritz rubbed his jaw and his whiskers made a raspy sound.

"Duplex!" cried Amber. That's what had been in the back of her mind trying to come out. "Dr. Grant said Walcott lives in a duplex."

"Like that one?" asked Fritz, pointing ahead.

She grabbed his arm. "That's it! See the Chevy! And there's a light on inside. See the mud on the plate? Oh, dear God, we found it." Tears welled up in her eyes. "Stop here and let's go in."

"Wait a minute. We can't just break in, you know. Walcott has rights the same as the rest of us."

She turned on Fritz, her eyes blazing. "Don't talk like a cop! I don't care right now. I care about the little girl in that house."

"Dr. Grant could've been wrong, you know."

Amber shuddered. "I know. But he could be right. I'm going inside. The last girl he raped is still in a clinic and her mind is gone. I won't take a chance on that happening again."

He ran a large finger around his collar, his face red. "We'll call the police later."

"Thanks. I mean it."

He pulled to the curb and Amber slipped out. She leaned down to whisper, "I'll knock on the door and say that I need to use the phone, that I ran out of gas. You stay back and watch in case he makes a break for it."

Fritz nodded, his body tense. A dog barked and in the distance a horn honked. "You be very careful, Red. Walcott's not known to be dangerous, but we don't know that."

"I'll be careful. You too."

He nodded.

She walked up the driveway to the side door. Wind tangled her hair. She opened the screen and knocked on the door. A curtain covered the glass part of the door and she couldn't see in.

Inside the kitchen Sam froze where he stood at the refrigerator. Who would be here this time of morning? Had someone heard Ann scream?

Ann jumped up, but before she could move Sam grabbed her and hauled her to the bedroom, pushing her inside. He heard a louder knock. Quickly he hooked the chain around Ann's ankle and clicked the padlock, then ran back to the door.

Amber wanted to smash in the glass and unlock the door but knew she had to be patient. She knocked again. Her knuckles hurt and she rubbed them against her jeans.

Sam shivered and looked helplessly around. Had Momma found out his new address? Had she come to check up on him? He pressed his face close to the door and said, "Who's there?"

Amber's stomach tightened. "I'm out of gas. I saw your light. Can you help me?"

He laughed in relief. It wasn't Momma after all, only some stupid woman who had run out of gas. Sam moved the curtain aside and peeked out. The woman looked tired and her hair was a mess. She couldn't be trouble for him. He opened the door but blocked it so she couldn't step in.

"I ran out of gas," said Amber. "Could I use your phone to call for help?"

"I don't have a phone."

"Do you have a can of gas? Just enough to get me to the station?" She peeked around him. The room seemed empty.

Something on the floor caught her attention. It was a bear, a tiny teddy bear. Her pulse leaped.

"I can't help you. The gas station is only a block away. You can walk there for help."

Suddenly Amber pushed Sam aside and walked right into the kitchen.

"Hey!" cried Sam. "What do you think you're doing?"

"I want to look around."

"Get out of here before I call the police." Sam grabbed for her arm, but she jumped away and almost knocked over a chair.

"You touch me and I'll scream so loud the whole neighborhood will wake up. Do you want that?"

Sam stared at the wild red-headed woman. "Are you crazy?"

Amber picked up the tiny bear. "Where did you get this?"

He looked at it in surprise.

Amber closed her hand over the bear and ran toward the closed door off the living room. Sam followed and caught at her arm but she shrugged him off. Amber flung the door open and Ann ran toward her, the chain rattling. "Ann!" cried Amber.

Sam fell back against the wall. The woman knew his Ann! What was going on here?

"Ann, I came to take you home to your mom and

dad," said Amber as she pulled Ann to her. "I'm Amber Ainslie and they hired me to find you."

Sam ducked out of the room and ran for the open kitchen door. Fritz stood just outside and Sam stopped short.

"You're under arrest, Walcott," said Fritz.

Sam burst into tears.

Fritz shoved Sam back inside. "Amber," Fritz called.

"In the bedroom. With Ann Hewitt. She's chained to the bed. Find a padlock key and bring it to me.

Fritz pushed Sam to a chair. "Where's the key?"

Sam pulled it from his pocket and meekly held it out to Fritz.

Several minutes later Ann sat at the kitchen table with the bear in her hands while Fritz waited for the Freburg police to come. Amber stood at the window and silently thanked God for His help.

After the police left with Sam, Fritz led Amber and Ann to his car and drove back to Bradsville. Ann sat quietly in the back seat, holding her bear.

When they reached Baker Street she bounced to the edge of the seat and cried, "That's my house! That's my dad's car!"

"The house is dark," said Amber. "It looks like they're still asleep. We'll ring the doorbell. They won't mind being woke up."

Fritz parked his car behind Morgan's. He winked at Amber and she smiled at him.

Ann scrambled from the car and ran to the door.

Amber touched Fritz's arm. "We did it, Fritz."

Around the lump in his throat he said, "We did it, Red."

She laughed as she followed Ann to the door. "Ring the doorbell, Ann."

Ann pressed her finger to the button and held it. From inside she heard the special chime it made. "I'm home," she whispered. "I'm home."

Chapter 14

Morgan sprang upright in bed. "Someone's at the door," he said. He jerked on his jeans.

"Could it be Ann?" asked Leta as she jumped from bed and pulled on her robe.

They ran to the door and flung it open, then stared in surprise at Ann.

"I'm home," she said. "And you're home too, Dad."

"Ann!" Morgan lifted her high in his arms and hugged her tight while tears rolled down his cheeks.

Leta wrapped her arms around both of them and cried great racking sobs.

Amber led Fritz to the kitchen and they sat at the table. She smiled at him and he smiled back. Happy voices drifted from the living room.

"You should go home and get to bed, Red."

"You too."

"I'll take you home first. After we stop for breakfast."

"I can't eat. But I'll watch you eat." She glanced toward the living room. "They'll have some questions once they settle down."

"I know." Fritz rubbed his eyes. "That was one long night."

Amber nodded.

In the living room Morgan dialed his parents

while he kept his eyes on Leta and Ann sitting together on the couch. Ann was talking about Sam Walcott. John Hewitt answered on the first ring.

"Dad. She's home."

"Thank God." John said to Dolly. "She's home."

Dolly grabbed the phone. "Morgan, is she all right?"

"Yes."

Dolly burst into tears.

John took the phone back. "We'll be right there."

Morgan hung up and said, "Leta, do you want to call your parents or shall I?"

"I will."

Morgan lifted Ann in his arms while Leta dialed her parents. "Mom and I are back together for good, Ann," said Morgan.

"Oh, Daddy. I knew it!" She hugged his neck hard.

Wanda answered the phone on the third ring.

"Mom, she's home," cried Leta.

Wanda dropped the phone and shouted, "Burl, she's home! Ann's home."

Burl ran in and scooped up the phone. "She's home?"

"She's home, Daddy."

"We'll be right over," he said. He didn't care if he was late for work. He didn't care if he went to work at all today.

Morgan walked to the window with Ann in his arms. He looked out at the neighborhood just waking for the morning. Leta touched his arm.

"Morgan, I want to call Sally."

He nodded. "Do."

"I told Sally I could walk to school by myself," said Ann in a tiny voice. "I did it too. Then Sam stopped me and talked to me and lied to me. He said he was taking me to see you, Dad, but he wasn't."

"You're with me now, Annie."

"I'm glad. I hope you're not mad at Sally. She wanted to go shopping real bad and I didn't want her to stay home just because of me."

"It's okay," said Leta as she let the Perrin's phone ring and ring.

A sleepy voice said, "Hello."

"Sally?"

"No, it's Deb."

"Deb, this is Leta Hewitt. Ann's home and safe."

"I'm so glad!"

"I want to tell Sally."

"I'll get her." Deb dropped the phone and ran to Sally's room. "Sally. Wake up. Ann's back! She's safe!"

Sally forced her eyes open, but she was too groggy from the sleeping pills to speak.

Deb pulled Sally up and shook her by the shoulders. "Leta wants to talk to you."

Sally flopped back on her pillow.

Suddenly Deb saw Sally's condition. "Oh, Sally." Deb ran back to the phone and said, "Leta, I can't wake her up. I'll have her call you later. Thanks for calling. Thanks a lot!" Deb hung up, reached in her nightstand and pulled out the sleeping pills. Most of them were gone. She dropped the bottle into the wastebasket and walked to Sally's room to be with her.

At the Hewitts, Amber and Fritz answered all of Morgan's and Leta's questions. Suddenly Amber yawned. "I'm sorry, but I've been up all night. We both have."

Fritz stood and pulled Amber up with him. "If you have any further questions, call later today and we'll answer. But right now we have to go. I'm glad you got your little girl back."

Amber kissed the top of Ann's head. "Talk to you later."

"Thank you, Amber," said Morgan, holding her hand with both of his.

"Yes. Thank you very much," said Leta. "We can never repay you for what you did."

Amber smiled and walked out with Fritz. In the car he lifted his brow questioningly. "How about breakfast?"

She nodded. "I'm tired but I couldn't sleep yet."

He drove to a quiet place where he ordered hashbrowns, eggs, bacon, toast and coffee for him. Amber wanted just tea.

Several minutes later she pushed back her cup and said, "Do you know what I need, Fritz?"

"Ten hours of sleep."

"Besides that."

"What?"

"A hot fudge sundae."

He laughed. "You've got to be kidding." He lifted his hand for the waitress. When she walked over he said, "Two hot fudge sundaes."

"With plenty of nuts," said Amber. When the waitress left Amber whispered, "Sundaes are a weakness of mine."

Fritz grinned. "Any weakness of yours is a weakness of mine."

Her eyes sparkled and she laughed. "You'd better watch out, Sheriff Javor, or I might jump into that long line of women after you."

He kept the smile glued to his face and sat very still. "I just might let you catch me."

"That'll be the day."

Later he drove her home and stopped outside her apartment. "I'll pick you up later to get your car."

"Thanks." She caught his big hand in hers. "You're a good friend. Thanks for your help. And breakfast. And the perfect sundae."

"You're beautiful, Red."

"So are you." Amber leaned over and kissed his cheek. "So are you."

Fritz watched her run to the door. He touched his cheek, then slowly drove away.

She walked into her apartment and stopped short. Mina lay asleep on the floor near the phone with a blanket wrapped around her. "Picked my lock again." Amber bent down and gently shook her. "Mina. I'm home."

Awkwardly Mina pushed herself up. "Did you find her?"

Amber nodded as she sank to the floor in front of her sound system. "She is home where she belongs. And he didn't rape her."

"What a relief!" Mina boosted herself up and sat on the love seat. She slipped on her glasses. "Now maybe you can take another case."

Amber groaned. "First let me catch up on some sleep."

"I will."

"It's been a long night. A long three days."

"But you do have a case to work on after that."

"Mina!"

"Don't get mad. Just listen to the man and you'll want to start right to work on it."

Amber kicked off her shoes and rubbed her feet. "Don't you ever mind your own business?"

"Not very often." Mina motioned to the tape player. "It's all on there. He stopped to see you and I took it all down for you. The man's young. Twenty-four. Married only a month and his wife disappeared. It's real sad."

Amber laughed. "You are a wonder, Mina Streebe."

"Do we take the case?"

"We?"

Mina shrugged.

"Do you know anything about computers?"

"I took classes."

"Is there anything you don't know?"

"Not much." She pushed her glasses up on her nose. "What do you have in mind?"

"Go to my office and check the hospitals, the morgue. You know the routine, I'm sure."

Mina nodded.

Amber picked up a notepad and scribbled a note to Carol. "Give this note to Carol, my secretary, and she'll let you have access to my office. Tell her we found Ann."

"Does this mean we're going to work together on this case?"

Amber sighed. "I guess it does. And Mina, while you're in town, would you go to the Buick garage and tell them to fix my taillights? Call Dr. Grant and tell him we found Ann and that Sam Walcott has been arrested. And keep looking for a country estate for me."

"Does this mean I'm going to work for you?"

Amber nodded hesitantly.

"Do I get paid? It's only fair, you know."

Amber tugged her shirt out of her jeans. "Tell Carol to put you on the payroll." She named a wage and Mina frowned. "Take it or leave it."

"I'll take it for now but, when you see how much help I'll be, you'll want to double that."

Amber picked up a pillow and tossed it at Mina. She ducked out the door before it could hit her. Amber tipped back her head and laughed.